D0969802

OCEAN WAVES

A QUILTING MYSTERY

OCEAN WAVES

TERRI THAYER

**WHEELER
CHIVERS**

LIBRARY OF CONGRESS CATALOGING-IN-PUBLICATION DATA

Thayer, Terri.
   Ocean waves / by Terri Thayer.
      p. cm. — (Wheeler Publishing large print cozy mystery) (A quilting mystery ; no. 3)
     ISBN-13: 978-1-4104-1786-2 (pbk. : alk. paper)
     ISBN-10: 1-4104-1786-7 (pbk. : alk. paper)
     1. Quilting—Fiction. 2. Murder—Investigation—Fiction. 3. Santa Clara Valley (Santa Clara County, Calif.)—Fiction. 4. Large type books. I. Title.
PS3620.H393O37 2009b
813'.6—dc22
                                       2009017530

BRITISH LIBRARY CATALOGUING-IN-PUBLICATION DATA AVAILABLE

Published in 2009 in the U.S. by arrangement with Midnight Ink, an imprint of Llewellyn Publications, Woodbury MN 55125-2989 USA.
Published in 2010 in the U.K. by arrangement with Llewellyn Worldwide Ltd.

U.K. Hardcover: 978 1 408 45710 8 (Chivers Large Print)
U.K. Softcover: 978 1 408 45711 5 (Camden Large Print)

ACKNOWLEDGMENTS

This is a work of fiction. The Asilomar in this book, while bearing a strong resemblance to the Refuge by the Sea, is a bit distorted. There are no hidden buildings, no secret walkways, except in my imagination. At least none that the state of California will cop to.

Thanks to the California State Park Rangers, especially Ranger Jacobus, for their time and patience. The mistakes, and liberties taken, are mine and mine alone.

To Jean Dunn, whose retelling of an apocryphal story about a missing woman at a quilting class got me thinking.

To Linda Stemer, the Blueprint on Fabric lady, for her brainstorming. We had fun conjuring up images.

Again thanks to Becky Levine and Beth Proudfoot. Their ability to read my rough drafts and tell me what I'm writing about is amazing.

To all the women of Asilomar, past, present and future.

OCEAN WAVES

Quilters have been making Ocean Waves quilts for over a hundred years. The block consists of small half-square triangles surrounding a plain block. The intriguing use of negative space is especially noticeable in

two-color quilts, but scrappy versions work well, too.

ONE

"I heard a woman scream," I said, for the second time. It was just after three in the morning. Buster had picked up on the first ring, answered in his cop voice, but now was drifting away. I needed him to listen to me.

"It wasn't me, I'm seventy miles away," Buster teased sleepily. My boyfriend delighted in getting me to make weird noises.

I shivered in the night air. The only pay phone I'd seen had been on the outside wall of the social hall, a quarter-mile away from my room. I'd hightailed it over here, slipping on my UGG slippers, but not grabbing a sweatshirt. Thankfully, I'd dragged my old quilt along. I pulled it tighter around my shoulders.

A cool breeze was blowing straight off the Pacific Ocean. I wasn't close enough to see it, but I could hear the waves breaking.

"A long, drawn-out scream," I continued

in my best I'm-not-kidding-voice.

"Even I'm not that good," he said. He was, but I wasn't on the phone to feed his ego.

"Funny, Buster. I'm serious. It sounded like it was coming from right outside my window."

"Don't be scared. It was probably a raccoon."

I shuddered. He knew I hated the little bandit rats that raided my home garbage cans at will. A scraping noise outside in the darkness made my heart race. In the dim light cast by the pole lamp, I saw a squirrel run up a tree.

I scrunched up my feet and moved closer to the building. The stone was little comfort. Putting the receiver back up to my ear, I heard Buster singing.

"What are you doing?" I asked.

"You've heard of 'Muskrat Love,' haven't you?" Buster said. Now I recognized the Captain and Tennille song. "What you heard last night was raccoon love."

"Bus-ter!" I raised my voice, then thought better of it. Noise carried in the dark. I didn't want to wake up my fellow quilters. Certainly not the seminar coordinator, Mercedes Madsen.

I whisper-warned, "Buster."

"I thought you liked it when I serenaded you. What time is it anyway?"

"Midnight," I lied. I was wide-awake. Alone. And far from home. I didn't want him to hang up.

His voice was strong and reassuring. "Dewey, babe, you're not in San Jose. Asilomar is a wildlife preserve. Animals make weird noises. That's all you heard."

"You think?" I said, my fear diminishing. I hadn't been sure what had woken me up, but I was sure he was the first person I wanted to tell.

I was attending the Sewing-by-the-Sea Symposium at Asilomar Conference Grounds in Pacific Grove, California. Five days of study with an internationally known quilt teacher. Five days to try to find ways to connect with my quilting customers the way my banished sister-in-law had. I'd bet the tuition, nearly fifteen hundred dollars, that this experience would fast track me to regaining ground I'd lost in my shop.

I realized Buster wasn't completely up to speed. I hadn't spoken to him since registration yesterday. I had to clue him in. "I'm going to be out of pocket this week. I had to turn in my phone."

"What do you mean?" Buster said. I heard his sheets rustle and wished I was there, under them.

"No cells allowed. We're allowed to use the pay phone during the evening hours, but that's it. Mercedes Madsen, the head honcho, collected them. Says they're a distraction that interferes with the learning process. I'm not even supposed to be on the phone now."

"How does she feel about visitors?"

"We're not supposed to have them."

Buster wasn't taking this too seriously. "Maybe this Mercury person has a conjugal room set up, like at the jail?" he teased.

"Mercedes," I corrected. "Don't give her any ideas. She might have been a prison guard in another life. She's a little too happy bossing people around."

I thought about my tiny sleeping room in the historic Stuck-up Inn. The bed, advertised as a double, took up most of the floor space. I tried to imagine Buster in there. At 6'4", he would have difficulty fitting on the mattress.

Spreading Buster catty-cornered on the bed in my mind, I asked, "When are you coming down?"

"I'll come down Wednesday night. I'm an expert at covert ops, you know. I majored in sneaking into dorm rooms in college."

It was Sunday, well, Monday morning.

That meant nearly three full days with no Buster. My heart sunk. "Not before then?" I said, unable to hide the disappointment. "I need some diversion."

"You know how much I love to divert you," Buster said huskily.

I felt my cheeks flame. Even after a year of dating, the sound of his voice could set off sparkly sensations in my belly. I squirmed in the phone booth, pushing the phone closer to my head as though I could feel Buster's breath on my ear.

"Tell me more," I said. "How exactly would you manage that?"

"Well, first I'd light the fire in your room, making it warm and toasty so your clothes feel too restricting. Then I'd take off your . . ."

"Stop!" A sharp voice cut into my reverie. I turned, tangling myself in the phone cord and nearly strangling myself.

Under the light, Mercedes Madsen stood with her hands on her hips. Her lips were pursed dangerously. She was fully clothed, despite the lateness of the hour. She looked extremely awake.

She reached past me and took the phone from me — along with a hunk of hair that was stuck in the cord. I jumped back, yelping in pain and outrage.

"What the heck are you doing?" I said, rubbing my sore scalp.

Mercedes spoke into the black receiver. "Ms. Pellicano will call you back this evening. Yes, she's fine. Just in violation of the rules. Thank you," she said in her clipped tones.

With a perfectly manicured finger, she hung up the phone.

Two

I could practically hear Buster laughing as she replaced the receiver in its holder. He would be getting a big kick out me being in violation.

Despite the night chill, I felt the sweat glands under my arms go into action, resulting in a damp sticky sensation I could have done without. Under the quilt, I held my arms away from my body. Mercedes looked at me strangely, and I tried to reduce the angle away from scarecrow down to marionette.

Of course, the woman standing in front of me was the epitome of organization and cosmetic coordination. Her sneakers were the same sea foam green as her sweat suit. Even at this hour.

I began to wish I'd shaved my legs this morning. And tweezed. The closer she got, the more I could practically feel my eyebrows growing toward each other, forming the world's bushiest unibrow.

"You're in Room 222? Correct?" she asked crisply.

I had to be impressed. There were probably three hundred students here. First she remembered my name. And now what room I was in? What was she, Super Woman?

At my quilt shop, Quilter's Paradiso, I could barely remember my most frequent customers. That had been Kym's forte. Kym, the sister-in-law I could not work with.

Mercedes raised her thin arm and looked at her bejeweled watch with great care. The dial was backlit with an eerie green light. I wasn't sure it didn't match the color of her sweatsuit.

"Phone privileges are allowed only between seven and nine p.m.," she said sternly.

"Sorry, it was an emergency," I said.

She grimaced. "Unless you're waiting for an organ transplant, there is no need to be on the phone except at the allotted times."

I looked at her stubbornly. I hated rules with no merit.

"You're not expecting a new heart or anything, are you?" she said sweetly.

She was the one that needed a new heart. Or maybe not. I hadn't seen evidence that she had one to begin with.

"No, but I heard a woman screaming," I said.

I expected some kind of reaction, but got none. She was looking at me with puzzlement but no alarm.

I wished there was more light so I could tell if she was really this calm. I glanced behind me. Inside, the registration desk was dimly lit. I could see an Asilomar employee behind the desk. I'd noticed the lack of activity as soon as I'd gotten here. Whatever I heard had not been enough to cause any upset.

"Some people mistake the mountain lion making its kill for a scream," she said easily.

My jaw dropped. "A mountain lion? There's a mountain lion on the loose?" I moved closer to the building, feeling the cold stone through the quilt. I steadied myself.

"Not exactly on the loose," Mercedes said dismissively. "There have been sightings in the area. Nothing to be concerned about. If you'd like, I can walk you back to your room."

I'd rather take my chances with a feline predator. "No thanks."

I waited to see if she'd move away from the phone, but she was protecting it as though it was the original Declaration of

Independence.

"I'll just go back to bed," I said.

"That's good," she said. "I need to have everyone in their room from midnight until six a.m. Otherwise, I'm in violation of my contract."

She called after me. "Breakfast begins at 7:30. I suggest you don't be late."

At 7:45 the next morning, I showed my meal ticket to the blue-vested woman at the door of the Crocker Dining Hall. I didn't want to miss food, but I couldn't bring myself to be right on time. Small victory.

Before coming here, I'd shot an e-mail off to Vangie. Surprisingly, despite our rustic surroundings there was free internet access in the small living room in the building I was staying in.

I'd woken up realizing I had a way around Mercedes' restrictions. Vangie and I had the laptop and the store computer configured with video conferencing. I told her in the e-mail that I'd call later, on my lunch break, to speak to her. I might look like an idiot talking to my computer in the middle of the wood-trimmed room, but at least I could touch base with her and find out what was going on at QP. Mercedes hadn't banished video.

Once I was inside the dining hall, a woman called to me from a table in the corner near the window. I threaded my way through the tables, many of them already filled with diners, mostly middle-aged women, with a few men sprinkled in. Half the tables were designated as reserved for the Sewing-by-the-Sea Symposium. The rest of the tables remained empty.

"Sit with us," an angular blonde in a striped sweater and jeans called, waving me over. I couldn't remember her name, but she shopped at QP. I was grateful to see a familiar, smiling face.

She speared a piece of French toast and pointed with it. "Move over, Nan."

I remembered her name now. Sherry Raney. She poured me a cup of coffee from the communal server, which I accepted gratefully. A lazy Susan sat in the center of the table, holding coffee pots, sugar, cups, and a pitcher of orange juice.

Nan was a chubby woman wearing a sweatshirt with a hummingbird that disappeared into the folds of her bosom. She grunted as she shifted slowly into the next seat. I sat down in her still-warm chair.

I nodded to the other nine people already seated. The women introduced themselves. Harriet Cohen and Lucy Lambrusco were from Long Island, another woman from Pennsylvania and another from Arizona. An auburn-haired beauty introduced herself as Red from Portland. Nan Orchard was from southern California. I didn't catch the rest.

"Dewey's our favorite shop owner," Sherry said to the others.

Lucy, a spiky-haired blonde wearing a New York Yankees sweat-shirt leaned in. Her hair complemented an elfin face. She was wearing a beaded choker with a small charm dangling on her freckled chest.

She said, "I love coming to the Bay Area. You have so many fabulous quilt stores."

Her friend with the out-of-control curly hair, Harriet, said, "I stopped in that shop in San Jose on my way here. Has that place gone downhill! No one greeted me when I walked in the door, and when I tried to get help with my supply list for class, the girl had no sense of color at all."

I reddened and Sherry shot me an apologetic look.

She started to speak, but the complainer wasn't finished. "Except when it came to her tattoos. *Those* were colorful."

A lump rose in my chest and my own little ankle tattoo felt aflame. Vangie was not every quilter's dream quilt shop employee. I loved her and she was invaluable to me, but what she was best at, the back office, was the stuff the customer never saw.

Sherry spoke loudly over the giggles. "Dewey owns Quilter Paradiso in San Jose."

Harriet sat back in her chair, looking slightly ashamed at her outburst.

Lucy patted my arm maternally. "Any shop can have a bad day," she said.

I smiled bravely. "We're working on our customer service. We've hired a new girl, and we're looking for more experienced people to work on the floor," I said.

Harriet didn't look appeased. I knew it didn't take much to ruin a quilt shop's reputation. My mother had told me a story of hearing someone trash one of the local shops when she was at Quilt Market in Pittsburgh. Twenty-five hundred miles away and the negative comments still came.

"Give us another try. I'll give you a special discount card," I said, reaching in my backpack for my business cards.

"What happened to Kym?" Lucy asked. "She was a big help to me when I bought the fabric for my Snow Pals quilt."

All the voices quieted. Red nudged Lucy, and whispered in her ear. It was common knowledge in certain quilting circles that I'd fired my sister-in-law, but word must not have reached the East Coast. Sherry watched for my reaction.

I felt a frown cross my face, and I struggled to keep smiling. My lips automatically turned down at the mention of my sister-in-law's name. I forced myself to look cheery, but I knew my eyes gave me away. Nan looked at me quickly and then went back to studiously buttering her sweet roll. She seemed sympathetic.

"She doesn't work for me anymore," I said quickly, hoping to quash any speculation. If anyone asked me what my sister-in-law was up to, I'd have to plead ignorance. I'd seen Kym exactly three times in the last six months. Thanksgiving, Christmas, and New Year's Day.

Red said, "I'm going to get my eggs. You hungry?"

Not anymore, but I pushed back my chair, eager to get away from the table talk about Kym.

For that, we had to line up and be served cafeteria-style. The hall that led to the kitchen window was lined with black-and-white photographs of Asilomar. I was entranced by the casual shots of smiling young women with bobbed hair.

Lucy came up behind me, nudged me, and pointed to the man who was punching tickets. "That guy has been with Asilomar since the fifties."

"The 1950s?" I said. I knew it sounded dumb, but the man greeting us didn't seem old enough to have worked here for nearly sixty years. He was white-haired, and had the wrinkled brown-paper-bag skin that attested to working in the sun, but his eyes were sparkling and he was warmly gracing each of us with a smile.

"Carlos," Lucy said. "Meet Dewey. A virgin."

I shot Lucy a look, but Carlos acted as though he'd heard it before.

"My pleasure, young lady. Enjoy your breakfast. If you have any questions about the facility, please ask me."

"My brother, Tony, is just starting to work here as a Ranger," I told him proudly.

"Then you won't be needing my personal tour. You've got your own guide," he said, returning my meal ticket and reaching past me to the next person in line.

"Carlos knows where all the bodies are buried," Lucy said.

Carlos frowned and waved his hand in a get-along motion. "No bodies, no secrets, no lies."

Carlos was finished with us, moving on to the people behind us, pushing us through the line. I got my plate filled with scrambled eggs, sausage, and biscuits and sat back at the table.

Once we were all settled, everyone was careful not to talk quilt shops.

"So, you're all friends?" I asked.

Sherry said, "We only see each other once a year, so we like to check in at mealtimes. We're hardcore. Been coming since the beginning. Fourteen years."

"Are you all in the same class?" I asked.

"Nah," Sherry said. "I'm in *Stars and Bars.*"

They spoke in turn around the table, naming the sessions they'd be attending. *Portraits in Fabric, Piecing Precision, Printing on Fabric,* and *Legendary Quilts.*

"What about you?" Nan asked. "What class are you taking?"

"I'm in *Legendary Quilts,*" I said.

Lucy gave a little wave, acknowledging that we'd be in class together. "Me too," she said. "And Harriet."

Harriet forced a smile.

"It's going to be a great week." Sherry said. "Mercedes always has a few surprises in store for us. Special exhibits, speakers."

"Strippers?" An older woman in a lacy cardigan cupped her ear and leaned across the table. "Did you say strippers?"

Nan said, horrified, "No, no, Rosie. No

need to worry."

"Who's worried? I just wanted to make sure I had dollar bills on me," she said, her skinny fingers rifling through the fanny pack strapped around her waist.

Sherry said, "Nan, you have an exhibit here, don't you?"

Nan nodded. "I brought some of my best sewing boxes. Mercedes is going to set them up in the chapel in time for the orientation meeting later."

"What meeting?" I asked.

Sherry said, "Oh, you'll be there. All Mercedes' meetings are mandatory. According to Mercedes, there are only three places her students should be in the evenings." She put up a finger for each item as she counted. "In a dorm sleeping, in a classroom sewing, or in the chapel at the scheduled event."

"Or on the phone. From seven to nine p.m.," I recited.

Lucy tilted her coffee cup in my direction. "Forget that. Bitsy Wong has that tied up. By the time she says good night to each of her eight kids, the time is up."

"Mercedes found me on the phone . . ." I started to tell them about my excursion last night until I realized I'd have to explain what I was doing out at three in the morning, and decided to drop my story. I wasn't ready to tell these women I'd thought I'd heard someone screaming in the night.

Still, I didn't understand how they put up with Mercedes' rules.

"How do you reach home while you're here?" I asked.

"I'm thrilled to be without my phone," Harriet said. "I'm on call all the time for my job, and this is the only time I can really relax."

"My kids bug their father for a change. Okay by me," Sherry drawled.

The redhead pointed her fork at Sherry, as if to start to say something, a piece of spinach from her omelet stuck on her front tooth. One of the others mimed scrubbing at her teeth until the redhead got the idea, and used her tongue to clear it before speaking.

"Is the Ghost in your class?" she said, finally.

"You mean she *isn't* in my class, don't you, Red?" Sherry said.

"I didn't see her at registration," Nan said, checking around the table.

My curiosity got the best of me. "Who's the Ghost?"

"She comes every year, from somewhere on the East Coast."

Lucy, the blonde, interrupted. "Vermont,"

she said.

At the same time, a round-faced woman broke in, "Indiana." She shrugged. "That's what I remember."

"We know what your memory is worth," Lucy said. That got a laugh. Everyone at the table was middle-aged, at least. I knew from my customers that they were sure to suffer from an impossible-to-rely-on brain.

"But who is the Ghost?" I asked.

"No one knows," Sherry said.

The redhead waved her fork again, spraying the ones nearest to her with bits of egg. "The point is, she comes every year, but attends class only on the first day, for maybe three hours. Until the first lunch hour, and then she disappears for the rest of the week."

But Sherry had a similar thought. "She might have met with foul play."

"She comes back every year," Nan offered as proof that she was still alive.

Red smirked and said, "I haven't seen her lately."

I thought about the scream I'd heard last night. Could that have been her?

I looked around the table. There were no signs of worry. I remembered that no one at the Administration building last night seemed concerned, either. I waited to see if anyone else brought it up. I was beginning to wonder if I'd dreamed the sound.

"What if *she's* a serial killer? 'She prowls the Monterey peninsula,' " Sherry said, doing a spot-on imitation of a movie trailer. " 'Quilting by day, killing by night. See the Sewing-by-the-Sea Seminar Killer, playing now in selected theaters. Gives a whole new meaning to the words Open Air Dyeing.' "

The women tittered, and Nan covered her mouth with her hand. Her eyes were dancing with delight.

"She's probably just catching up on her sleep," Lucy said. "One year Rachel Clark came and folded fabric the entire time. She said it was restorative."

"I'll tell you what's restorative . . ." Red offered, her voice, low and sexy. "A week holed up with a man."

"Sometimes she shows up for the last night show and tell," Nan said, talking over Red. "Looking great. Well rested."

"Well screwed is more like it," Red said.

Two quilters recoiled. Several laughed. I scooped up the last of my egg using my toast, hiding a smile. The quilters I knew could be salty, unlike their image portrayed on bathroom tissue commercials. And a murderous bunch.

"Seriously," Red continued. "What do you think she does for a week? She's shacked up somewhere with a guy."

"It's like that movie, *Same Time, Next Year,*" another person put in. Her eyes got soft. "Alan Alda, isn't he the sexiest man ever?"

I was more a Clive Owen or Jonathan Rhys-Meyer fan myself. Alan Alda was older than my father. Cute, but wicked old. Almost as old as James Garner.

Sherry said, "You know what they say: what happens in Asilomar stays in Asilomar."

"*Nobody* says that," Red said.

Conversation faded as the Ghost talk sputtered. No one knew much about her. I looked around the large room, hoping to find a new conversation topic. The bones of the room were my favorite style of architecture, Arts and Crafts style. The muslin drapes with pine cone stencils and overhead beams gave the huge place a cozy feel.

I knew my Arts and Crafts. "Julia Morgan was the architect here, wasn't she?" I said. "Do you know who she is? She was an Arts and Crafts proponent, famous here in the Bay Area."

I was getting blank looks. We were sitting in one of the best examples of this kind of architecture around. I couldn't believe no one cared.

"She did Hearst Castle?" I prompted, breaking off a piece of toast.

My unsuccessful attempt to change the subject was interrupted by a shrill, high-pitched noise. I clamped my hands over my ears.

Mercedes stood on a chair in the middle of the room, her hand still on the whistle around her neck. There was no need to blow it again. The air seemed to reverberate from the last blast. The room grew quiet. Even the gulls outside stopped crying.

Mercedes began. "By now, you should be getting settled at the fourteenth annual Sewing-by-the-Sea quilt symposium. I'm Mercedes Madsen, the one who will hear all of your complaints, large or small. I know you'll have some, you always do."

I was taken aback by her tone, as though she was admonishing a bunch of four-year-olds who had spilled their milk on the carpet and refused to stop playing in it. It wasn't just me she treated like a child. I bristled, but looking around, I saw only smiling faces. No one else seemed to mind.

Mercedes said, "No questions? No complaints about your roommate's snoring?" She looked around.

The noise in the room flattened even more. Most of the women watched Mercedes with affection. I felt like the only one who found her abrasive.

"In that case, I want to introduce Ranger Schmitt."

"Good morning," the smiling ranger said. Her friendly demeanor was in high contrast to Mercedes. This was a woman who enjoyed her work. And people.

I had a second reason for coming to this seminar. My brother, Tony, a California Park Ranger, had been assigned to Asilomar. This might be his boss up there.

"I welcome you. My rangers are at your disposal. We want you to have the best experience possible," she said warmly

The ranger continued, "Here at Asilomar, we co-exist with the local wildlife. That's why we ask you not to walk in the dunes, and to stick to the paths when you're moving between buildings. Respect the ecosystem and we'll all get along fine."

Ranger Schmitt stepped aside and Mercedes took over. "Good advice. Stick to the rules and we'll have a great week."

She looked around meaningfully. Some quilters bowed their heads, afraid to look her in the eye.

She continued, "For now, let me remind you of the parameters. Your classes are held from nine until four each day. Breakfast is at 7:30, lunch at noon, dinner at six. You can sew in the classrooms until midnight. Cell phones are banned as usual. I thank you in advance for cooperating," she said, pausing for effect and letting her gaze fall on me.

No one spoke. Mercedes continued, "One more thing. I'd planned to introduce you to my new assistant this morning, but she is feeling under the weather."

"Mini-Mer," Sherry whispered.

Mercedes said, "We're housed in the Pirates' Den. We have set up our office in the living room area. Feel free to stop by with your concerns."

She held her arms up, her voice rising like a preacher's.

"At Sewing-by-the-Sea, we believe that total immersion is the key to learning. This is why your linens are changed for you, your meals are provided, and your classrooms stocked with the latest technology. We will make every effort to make your lives trouble free."

She smiled, looking around the room. Her voice deepened.

"To that end, please limit yourself to the Asilomar grounds. I know many of you don't have your cars here, but those that do, I insist you abide by the rules. No trips off campus. I will collect car keys, if necessary."

I glanced at the others at my table, trying to gauge their reaction to this bombshell. The women were unconcerned.

Was that orange juice in that pitcher or Kool-Aid? I felt like I'd been dropped into a cult. No one at the table would look me in the eye. I resisted the temptation to look under the table and see if they were all wearing new sneakers.

"Back to class," Mercedes said, clapping her hands like a frontier schoolmarm. "Remember, no forays off the grounds. No exceptions."

THREE

I hurried out of the dining hall, my scrambled egg a lump in my stomach. I hadn't been without my keys since the day I'd turned sixteen and passed my driver's test. My car was a part of me. There was no way I was giving her my keys.

I didn't get past the porch. My older brother, Tony, was standing on the step, in full California State Park Ranger gear. I resisted the urge to punch his shoulder, settling for a gentle nudge with my elbow.

Tony had just been assigned to Asilomar. I wondered how he would handle mentoring a bunch of middle-aged women. He was used to rougher terrain in the eastern Sierras.

He seemed to be doing okay, reassuring a pink-faced woman that she had not crushed an endangered wildflower by crossing on the dirt path through the circle of pines. She walked away, seemingly mollified.

He pulled me in for a hug. "Hey, sis."

Quilters passed us as they hurried off to class.

"Bro," I said, our usual greetings. "Enjoying your new gig?"

"It's different," he said, shrugging. "I've got a lot to learn."

"Yeah, I know. You know your wildlife and nature, but what about the history of this place? Which buildings are the Julia Morgan ones? How about the YWCA? Do you even know what a Stuck-Up is?" I quizzed him. I'd read everything I could about the place before coming down.

He had a blank look on his face. It wasn't often I knew more than my big brother. It felt good. I laughed. "You've got some reading to do. I've got some books you can borrow."

A bell tolled, signaling that class would begin in five minutes. My classroom was a bit of a walk, at least a half mile away.

"I've got to go," I said.

"Coffee later? I'm off at three," he said.

"Here? Not going to happen," I said. "The espresso machine is broken in the store." I knew the one thing Tony valued about civilization was good coffee.

"All right. Meet me in town. Juice 'n' Java."

The pink-faced woman laid a hand on Tony's arm. She had another question. He bent down to answer her.

"Make it four," I said. Class would be over by then. I wasn't supposed to go into town, but what could Mercedes do anyway? Kill me?

Tony waved me off, and said to her, "If you'd like to know more, you're welcome to join the nature walk at six tomorrow morning."

Six a.m. Yikes. Part of the ranger's duties here were informative sessions with the guests. Tony, as the newest arrival, must have pulled the early duty.

I hurried up the asphalt path leading through the pines. My head was down, deep in thought about Tony and what it would mean having him nearby for the first time in years. He'd been assigned all over the state, but never so close to home before.

He'd left home for college when I was about fourteen. Fourteen and so engrossed in my own circle of friends, I'd barely noticed when he'd gone. But I hadn't known then his choice of profession, or maybe his nature, would keep him far from the family for years. He and I had a lot of catching up to do.

Asilomar was a state park, policed by

California Park Rangers. I didn't know if Tony had chosen this gig, or if it had been forced on him. His previous stints had been in wilderness areas.

Asilomar was a series of unconnected buildings, hidden among the pine trees and scrub oaks. It was bordered by the ocean, the town of Pacific Grove and the resorts at Pebble Beach. Built as a women's retreat by the YWCA in the early part of the twentieth century, newer buildings had gone up fifty years later.

According to the map I'd been given in my registration packet, my classroom, Evergreen, was on the opposite side of Asilomar Road, past the bog and the native-stone pillars built nearly a hundred years ago. The building was small, just the size of a classroom. The walls were wood with plenty of windows. A piano sat next to the door and a large fireplace dominated the opposite wall.

Two six-foot tables sat in the middle of the room. The rest of the tables were positioned around them in a square so that when seated, the students would face the teacher in the middle and see each other. I found an empty space, and laid down my tote bag. Beaded, painted, decorated with found objects and fancy couched yarns, one

37

of my favorite customers, Pearl, had made it for me. The pocket was embellished with a pithy question: "What is not art?"

The perimeter of the room was ringed with colorful rolling carts and tote bags. Mercedes had collected our bags at registration. She or her assistant must have parked them in here since last night. I had to wonder what kind of woman her assistant was. Someone who didn't mind being bossed around?

Several students had the expensive Tutto bags. We'd just started carrying them at the store. Coming in bright colors, like lime green and hot pink, they were sturdy enough to go on an airplane. Even at cost, I couldn't afford one right now. I retrieved my plain-Jane suitcase filled with fabric and supplies.

The teacher was pinning small quilts to the wall, which was covered in burlap between the wood battens. She was dressed in many layers of earth-toned clothing. She was wearing scarves and what looked like more than one skirt, and several tank tops. A vest flapped open as she reached up, revealing the silk paisley lining. Her arm was covered in bracelets, and necklaces of all sizes coexisted on her neck.

I couldn't begin to understand how to dress like that, but she looked great —

feminine and ethereal, and definitely artistic.

The students filed in. I recognized Harriet from breakfast. She settled in next to me, dropping her huge purse on the table. It was pieced from a line of Moda fabric, all faded reds and blues, paisleys and flowers, held together with grommets the size of shower-curtain holes. I loved it.

"I'm glad to see a familiar face," I said, even though we'd just met.

"I'm sorry I brought up your sister-in-law this morning. I didn't know that was a sore spot," Harriet said.

"It's okay. You couldn't have known. She and I just didn't get along. We had very different views on how to run the business."

"I know how that is. Family businesses can be hard. My husband and my brother-in-law nearly came to blows over a small trucking business they had."

I was quiet for a moment. "Kym's the reason I'm in this class."

Harriet looked interested, so I continued. "I didn't know how to quilt. I inherited QP from my mother, and had to learn. When Kym left," I said. I took a breath and started again. "When I fired Kym, it left a gap in our staff. She was very popular with the traditional quilters. I'm trying to learn."

"This isn't exactly traditional quilting,"

Harriet noted, pointing toward the quilts on the walls. They had traditional elements but used fusible appliqué to tell a story.

"It's a compromise," I said. "My leanings are toward art quilts, so I'm hoping this class will blend the two."

Harriet gave me a look that said good luck. I swallowed my trepidation and smiled at her. Lucy sat down on the other side of Harriet and greeted me.

The teacher cleared her throat. All of the students looked her way.

"My name is Cinnamon Ramstad, the class is *Legendary Quilts,* and I'm here to frighten you."

An uncomfortable giggle went through the room. There were eighteen other students in the class. The lady across from me brought her finger to her lips and bit her cuticle.

"I'm terrified already," I said. I meant only for Harriet to hear but I'd spoken too loudly. The teacher came to the edge of my table, rapping her knuckles on the top. I jumped. She wasn't allaying my fears.

Silver bangles slid down her arm with a musical clang. "Don't be," she said.

I felt the need to explain. "I'm not a very accomplished quilter."

Cinnamon smiled and I felt less scared.

She had a maternal air that helped me feel okay.

"In this class, there are no quilt police. I'm not interested in your technique. I'm interested in your thoughts."

The class got quiet. Next to me, a woman took in a deep intake of air. I wasn't the only one who had doubts.

Cinnamon tossed her braid over her shoulder. She pulled herself up on her table, and let her legs cross. She folded her hands. She looked calm and serene, as if she was holding a yoga class.

"We're going exploring here. All I ask is that you keep your mind open and your heart clear," she said.

What had I gotten myself into? This seminar was nothing like I thought it was going to be. I felt my stomach do a flip. I wanted to call Buster, call Vangie, even Ina to talk this out, but with no cell phone, I was cut off.

A figure outside the window startled me. It was a doe, reaching up to pull a leaf off an oak tree. She jumped slightly as I watched. The sight calmed me down. This wasn't life or death after all. It was just quilting.

Cinnamon jumped down, and did a turn, including everyone in the room in her gaze.

"You might have come with some preconceived notions about what your legendary quilt will be. I want you to get rid of those right now. You need to discover what your theme will be. We will do an exercise that will help."

As she walked around the room, she laid a large piece of butcher paper on each desk. She told us to get out the markers she'd asked us to bring. When she was finished, she pushed a button on her Ipod speakers.

To my surprise, rock 'n' roll blasted through. I'd been expecting waterfalls or ocean-wave music. I bit back a laugh. Harriet, Lucy, and I exchanged grins.

Cinnamon continued, "Every map has a legend. You are going to create the legend to your quilt map. Take a marker and write down a word."

The entire class fingered their markers. We exchanged furtive glances. One woman cracked her neck loudly. Another blew her nose. Not one marker hit the page.

Cinnamon reached her hands up to the ceiling. "10, 9, 8 . . . One word, people. One."

Someone coughed nervously.

"3, 2, 1. Go," Cinnamon yelled.

Markers squeaked and the smell of the

ink filled my nose. We all scratched down a word.

"Pens up," the teacher said. "Now I'm sure you think your word is banal. Totally lame."

She waited for our murmurs of agreement to die down.

"You're right," she said. She smiled a crooked smile. "Most first thoughts are. Don't worry; we'll get to the good stuff."

She made us stand and take several deep cleansing breaths. Her braid touched the floor as she bent from the waist. When she thought we were fully oxygenated, she asked us to pick up our pens again.

"Now, using balloons, make connections to your first thought. Random thoughts. Single words, phrases. Quickly, without stopping to think. I'm going to give you ten minutes to brainstorm. Don't overthink this. In fact, if you can not think at all, that would be better."

I heard my brothers' collective voice saying that shouldn't be a problem.

I looked at my page; blank except for one word.

When I'd signed up for the class, I'd thought that I would do a quilt about my remodeling project, so I wrote down "House." Now I connected Buster to the house, and proceeded to add words like wood, family, dog, yard. I had no idea where this was going, but so far it was pretty mundane.

I got stuck after those five words. I looked around at the heads down. Everyone seemed to be writing diligently.

Most of the women taking the classes were older than I was. Not surprisingly, many quilters are. It takes time and money to be a dedicated quilter, especially to take a week away from family and or job, and spend fifteen hundred dollars on what might seem like an indulgence, a week of quilt classes with a famous teacher.

People with small kids, like Jenn, who worked for me at QP, couldn't take a week off to attend a quilting class, no matter how understanding the man they were married to. Jenn had real envy about my coming down here, and I felt a desire to make her and the rest of the people at the store proud of me. Ina, Vangie, and Jenn were all working extra shifts so I could be here. I forced my mind back to the task at hand.

I wrote wainscoting, beadboard, pedestal sink. It was turning into a wish list for Home Depot. Not what Cinnamon was looking for.

After a few more minutes than I needed

of quiet time, Cinnamon asked for a volunteer to pin her response up on the easel she'd set up.

Lucy raised her hand. Her first word had been Asilomar. She pointed to the bubbles that surrounded her initial input.

"My great-grandfather worked here in the twenties and thirties," she explained. "He left pictures to my mother. I'm using copies of them, as a jumping-off point. I have her diaries, and letters, too. I thought this was the right place to work on an Asilomar quilt."

"Has the brainstorm done anything to change your mind?" Cinnamon asked. "Did you discover anything new?"

She looked at the board. "I'd thought it was going to be all sepia tones and lace, but now that I'm here, I'm thinking I'll make it more naturalistic, with images of the ocean, sky, and trees."

"Great," Cinnamon said. "You've expanded your horizon. Literally." She clapped her hands. "Time for lunch."

After lunch, we critiqued each other's quilt maps. I enjoyed the process far more than I thought I would, hearing about the stories behind each quilt.

When it was my turn to speak, we were

interrupted by the sound of a chime. Cinnamon glanced at her watch.

"Oh, I knew the day would just fly by. We've got to break for now. The room will be open this evening after orientation until midnight. I'll be here later for questions."

Even though I was glad I didn't have to talk about my quilt, I was surprised to feel a twinge of disappointment. I was actually sorry to see the class end.

Cinnamon raised her voice to be heard above the scraping of chairs, and said, "Your homework assignment tonight is to answer this question: What are you running away from? Sometimes the thing you're trying to leave behind is exactly what you need."

I had agreed to meet Tony for coffee, so I found my car and drove the short distance into Pacific Grove. I felt slightly dazed from the first day of class. I'd never spent that much time on one quilting task. My mind kept working on the story I wanted to tell, about the store and my family, but I was happy to be on my way to see my brother. It had been too long.

Of course, my grabbing my car could be seen as a running away of sort. Was I beginning to think like Cinnamon? That was a funny thought.

The shopping district was only about four blocks long, with a grassy strip up the middle. Pedestrian walkways bisected the road, so I had to drive slowly. A parked car, driven by a blue-haired woman, pulled out without warning. I slammed on my brakes, heart set to pounding. The woman drove off without realizing I'd nearly hit her.

I parked in a spot in front of a small diner. A slightly chubby policeman in a wheelchair passed me, chalking my tires, enforcing the two-hour parking limit.

Pacific Grove touted itself as America's Hometown, and the nickname was well suited. The small town perched on a hill overlooking one of the most scenic stretches of the western coastline, its main street was lined with art galleries, antique stores, and funky restaurants. Buster and I'd been down here for the Good Old Days festival last year and had fallen in love with the place.

There was no sign of Tony, even though I was a few minutes late. I ordered a vanilla latte and sat down at one of the tables. *The Pacific Grove Hometown Bulletin,* the local newspaper, was spread out on the table in front of me. The front page caught my eye.

The headline read, "She sounds just like a damsel in distress." I pulled the paper closer. The article was about the mountain lion that had been seen close to Asilomar's grounds two nights earlier. Residents were warned not to travel alone at night and to call the game warden if they spotted her. I devoured the article, glad to know I wasn't the only one who'd heard screams late last night.

That led me to the police blotter. Whoever wrote it had an enjoyable sense of ironic humor that took the sting out of the car burglaries and neighbor noise complaints. I was so engrossed that I didn't realize how quickly the time was going. I glanced at the clock on the wall. Twenty minutes had passed. And no sign of Tony.

Where was he? I sipped the last of my latte. I couldn't really linger, not with Mercedes on the warpath. I was bummed out. I'd really wanted to spend some time with my brother.

I hadn't seen him since the anniversary sale at the shop. That day had gone by in a flash — I'd barely said hello to him. The next morning, he was back in the mountains, searching for wayward hikers.

This gig at Asilomar meant he'd be closer to home than he had been in years. I wanted to be sure he came into San Jose for Sunday suppers at Dad's, Sharks' games, and

Wednesday basketball night. I wanted to make sure he was going to be part of the family again.

But I couldn't wait any longer. The five o'clock orientation and viewing of the sewing boxes was not to be missed. I'd just clicked my car open when a man approached me.

"You're a quilter?" he asked. His voice was deep, but friendly. He had a nice smile, the skin crinkling around his eyes as though he smiled a lot. He was middle-aged, somewhere younger than my dad, but older than me. His brown hair was gray at the temples and his eyebrows were tufting uncontrollably over his brown eyes. "Are you taking a class at Sewing-by-the-Sea?"

"What gave me away?" I said, checking out my clothes. No pieced vests, no threads on my sweatshirt, no cute sayings like "Old quilters never die, they just go to pieces" on my T-shirt. Nothing that screamed, "I'm a quilter."

"I took a wild guess." He pointed at the Quilter Paradiso logo splashed across my car door.

"Oh, that." Vangie had insisted on outfitting me with a magnetic sign with the store info on it. I wasn't sure that advertising on my old Honda didn't send a mixed message. Great business, but not so successful that I could buy a new car.

"You're on to me," I said.

"You're awfully young to have a quilt shop," he said, smiling.

It was true. I was the youngest quilt shop owner in California. I felt flattered that he'd noticed.

"Young and pretty."

I blushed. "Do you quilt?"

I knew better than to assume a guy didn't sew.

"Me? That's a good one," he said, chortling. "No. My wife is the quilter in the family. Ursula."

I could see the ocean downhill over his head. His hair was being swept off his face by the same wind that ruffled the ocean waves. He sounded like a New Englander, perhaps an ancestor of one of the Methodists that had founded Pacific Grove a hundred years ago.

"I'm Paul Wiggins, by the way. From Lowell, Mass," he said.

I'd guessed right. He held out his hand for me to shake. His palm was soft but his grip was hard. He held my hand for a second, and looked into my eyes. His eyebrows were charming.

"Dewey Pellicano," I said. "Is your wife at

Sewing-by-the-Sea?"

"She is," he said, his eyes turned troubled. "I've been trying to reach her, without success."

Mercedes' silly ass rules. This guy missed his wife. Sweet. "The seminar director doesn't approve of outside distractions," I said, shrugging. Why was I apologizing for her?

"I know, I know." His eyebrows knitted, and he crossed his arms across his chest. He looked away, his eyes going unfocused.

"It's her mother," he said softly. "I got the news almost as soon as I dropped her off yesterday."

My throat clutched. "Her mother?" I had a soft spot for mothers, ever since mine had died so young a year and a half ago. "Did you leave a message at the Administration desk?" I asked.

"I tried that," he said. "But she hasn't called me, so I can only assume she hasn't gotten my messages."

"Well, I can let her know, if you'd like," I said, wondering as soon as the words were out of my mouth how I would find this Ursula Wiggins among the three hundred quilters that were attending the symposium.

"That would be grand," he said. "I'm sure she'd be forever grateful."

"Do you know what class she's taking? Which teacher?" I needed to narrow down my search options.

He tapped his teeth, as though trying to recall the specifics. "Hayden Van Susskind? Susanna Pierson?" He named several well-known quilters.

Now I'd done it. Committed myself to the proverbial needle in a haystack. A haystack guarded by Colonel Mercedes. I immediately wanted to take back my offer, but the look on his face was pitiful. His eyes slanted sadly and his hand trembled slightly. He stuffed the offending hand into his pocket.

"Her mother is asking for her," he said. "She's taken a turn for the worst since we left Boston. She's a native of Poland, and she's reverted to speaking only Polish. No one can understand her except Ursula."

My heart thumped. How lonely to be on your deathbed with no one around you to talk to. Who would she tell her final words? My eyes filled with tears. Buster had been with my mother when she died, comforting her. I treasured that thought.

"I've purchased a red-eye ticket for both of us. We need to get to the San Jose airport tonight. I'd hate to go home without her," he said morosely.

"Tell you what, Paul," I said, making up

my mind. Mercedes' rules were ridiculous. "I'll give you a ride onto the grounds. We'll find your wife together and you can tell her yourself. She can call her mother and you two can fly home."

FOUR

We drove the two miles back to Asilomar in silence, passing the large cemetery. I caught a glimpse of the ocean as I took the wide turn at the foot of Lighthouse Blvd. The whitecaps were stirred up.

I said, "My brother's a ranger. He might be able to help us find your wife."

"That's nice of you to offer," he said. "But I'll just wait until class is over and waylay her outside the dining hall."

I looked at the clock on the dashboard. It was going on 4:30. "That's nearly two hours from now," I said, then it came to me, "Oh wait, she'll be at the orientation meeting. Let's go there."

My heart ached for his mother-in-law. It was such a sad situation. I felt a flare of anger at Mercedes. It was one thing if she wanted her students to have privacy, but she had no business screening her students' calls and prohibiting visitors.

I parked in the lot nearest the Sand-and-Sea classroom. I'd barely gotten my door open when Mercedes came out of the Pirates' Den at a run. The building housed several sleeping rooms and a rustic living room that she was using as her headquarters.

She must have seen me pull in and was coming to harass me for using my car. I needed to take off the QP signs stat.

But she didn't look at me. Her mouth was a thin line, and her eyes were narrowed at Paul dangerously. "What's he doing here?"

I stopped, my door open, and looked across at Paul. He was already out of the car, smiling at Mercedes.

I tried to be polite. "Mercedes, have you met Paul? His wife, Ursula, is attending the conference. He's got a very important message to get to her."

Mercedes walked past me and headed straight for Paul. She pointed at him. "Get out of here. Now."

I was shocked at her demeanor. Mercedes' eyes were flashing, and she'd pulled herself up to her full five-foot stature. Her cheeks were pink and shiny.

She wasn't getting how desperate he was to talk to his wife. I closed my door and moved around to the passenger side. "Hold on a minute," I said. "Ursula's mother is sick and calling for her daughter . . ."

Mercedes didn't look at me. She was locked in gaze with Paul. He had the tiniest smirk on his face. My stomach churned. Something was not right.

Mercedes stopped, hands on her hips, one bony hip cocked. Her voice dripped with sarcasm. "Your wife's not here, Paul. She's not attending this year."

That stopped him. He looked genuinely perplexed. "Of course she is. She flew in yesterday. Don't lie to me."

Denying that she was even here was really going too far. "What's the problem, Mercedes? So he wants to talk to his wife."

"You don't get it. It's because of men like him . . ."

Paul guffawed. "Men like me? You hate the whole species, Mercedes. Admit it. You're a castrating bitch whose only power comes from picking on women who don't have the balls to stand up to you."

I stared at him. The conversation had taken another turn I hadn't seen coming. I took a step away from my car and closed the door. Paul's fists were clenched at his side, and his neck was red and blotchy. He had switched from reasonable to angry in a split second. I took a step back.

Mercedes, to my surprise, moved closer to Paul. She stood on her tiptoes, words coming out with such force that she was spitting.

"What are you going to do, Paul? Hit me?"

Paul retreated, his back now against my car. Mercedes continued to crowd him.

"Power? You want to talk to me about power? Did you tell Dewey that you beat your wife when she doesn't agree with you? When your dinner is late? If the lawn isn't mowed? That your power comes from your fists?"

Paul's eyes had gone cold. My stomach twisted, and I felt sick. I never should have let this guy sweet talk me into bringing him here.

"That's not true," he said.

Mercedes scowled. "I've known Ursula for years. We talk about things, Paul. We share. You have no idea what I know about your life. And you have no idea how your life is about to change."

Why had I been so ready to believe him? I think the idea of circumventing Mercedes' rules was too tempting to me. I'd assumed too easily, perhaps, that Mercedes was just being unreasonable.

Paul Wiggins talked to me, ignoring Mercedes. "Ms. Pellicano, please believe me when I say I didn't mean to get you in trouble. I have no intention of harming my wife. Mercedes doesn't know the first thing about the relationship my wife and I have. No one does. I'd like to tell you more about Ursula some time. Ours is an unusual love story, not readily understood."

Suddenly he stiffened. The light caught on something metal. I took my eyes off his face and looked at Mercedes.

She had produced a gun and was pointing it low at Paul's side. My knees shook. Was she going to kill him?

"Mercedes," I said. "Please —"

Without looking at me, she said, "Get out of here, Paul Wiggins. You're scum."

My mouth went dry. A gun. I looked around. The ocean continued to pound the shore. No rangers or Asilomar staff was in sight. No one but me to witness the small hunk of metal in Mercedes' hand.

"Mercedes, please, can't we talk this out?" I asked. My voice was scratchy and low. I didn't know if she heard me.

Paul looked at the tiny firearm in her hand, the smirk never leaving his face.

She didn't look short and petite right now. It wasn't just the presence of the gun. She seemed to have expanded like a Komodo dragon, with a ruff that doubled in size.

Mercedes said, "I will shoot you, Paul, if you set foot here again. I suggest you go back to the rat hole you crawled out of." Her voice was steady and calm, but her angry eyes flashed.

"I'm holding you responsible," he cried. He crawled back into my car.

Mercedes looked angrily at me, still pointing the gun at Paul. I shook my head. There was no way I was taking him back to Pacific Grove.

"Scram," Mercedes said, kicking my car door with her foot.

Paul got out of my car, cursing Mercedes as he went. She kept her gun trained on him.

He started out of the parking lot, walking toward the road. He turned. Mercedes gestured with the gun. "I'm not leaving Pacific Grove until I speak with my wife."

I didn't look at him, pretending not to hear. Paul Wiggins made me sick to my stomach. I couldn't shake the feeling that I'd let a snake loose in the hen house, as my Grandmother Dewey might have said.

But I had other things on my mind. I turned to Mercedes.

"A gun? You have a gun?" I said, my voice raising an octave.

"Settle down," she said. She put her arm down. "It's not real."

"Not real?" I rubbed the back of my neck. "What are you doing, flashing a fake gun around?"

"You have no idea what it takes to keep these women safe," she said to me. "That guy is nothing but trouble. Stay away from him."

She strode away from me, and disappeared into the door of her office. I stood, gaping at the spot where she'd just been.

She came back empty-handed, and snatched my keys from me. "I'll take those. You're grounded."

FIVE

I stomped up the hill toward the Administration building and my room. This place was nuts. Locked up women and their crazy-ass husbands. I was going to pack my bags and go home.

A seagull swooped down into the path ahead, tearing a potato chip out of a discarded bag.

I walked in a circle, standing on the edge of the path. The gull flapped away, then hopped back. The chips were too tempting for him to fly away.

I didn't know what to do. I wanted to leave, but the money I'd spent for the seminar would be wasted. I caught sight of someone coming toward me in a yellow, full-length coat. The sight stopped my heart for a moment. The wearer looked like a cross between Big Bird and the Grim Reaper.

Then, before I could scream or run, he

threw back the hood to reveal Freddy Roman, of Freddy's Fine Fabrics Emporium.

"Freddy," I said relieved, holding my arms out for a hug. Freddy's brand of humor and quick insight was just what I needed. He came close. I rubbed his shoulders, admiring the felted wool and purple braided trim. "I didn't know you were here."

I was glad to see him. I'd first met him at last year's Extravaganza, and we'd hit it off. His snarky sense of humor and tendency to gossip was just what I needed. He would understand my issues with Mercedes.

"You're about the last person I'd thought I'd see here," he said. "You're not much of a quilter, are you?"

That was Freddy, overly harsh in his assessments, but usually right on the money. He was the Simon Cowell of the quilt world.

"Trying to be. Why weren't you at lunch?" I hadn't seen him at breakfast either.

Freddy's eyes opened wide. His lashes were long. Too long to be natural. His pancake makeup didn't quite hide the old acne scars on his cheeks. For a straight man, Freddy spent a lot of money on clothes and cosmetics. But then, he lived in Los Angeles, where youth and beauty were the religion. Botox, the sacrament.

"New diet regimen," he said. "I'm getting

deliveries from a local restaurant. I eat only fresh pineapple until eleven a.m. After that, it's broccoli and pasta. Nothing but water after four. I've lost eleven pounds in two weeks. You should see the color of my poo."

I turned my head to stave off any more information. Freddy was as thin as anyone could want to be. Something he said piqued my interest. "You get delivery? Is that allowed under Mercedes' rules?"

"There are plenty of ways around our fearless leader," he said conspiratorially.

He stomped his pale yellow cowboy boots with fancy purple scrolling for emphasis.

"How are things in San Jose?" Freddy asked. "I saw some of your original patterns at Spring Market last month. Quilter Paradiso, oh pardon me, *QP,* was getting a lot of buzz."

I was trying to change the name of the store my mother had started. QP sounded edgier, hipper. Customers and people like Freddy that had known it for twenty years as Quilter Paradiso had trouble switching over.

I ignored his jab at my changes. "The store's doing okay. QP Online is thriving, although it takes up more of our time than Vangie and I had imagined."

If I was being completely honest, I'd have

told Freddy that I'd lost a base of customers, the hardcore traditional quilters, followers of Kym, when I'd fired my sister-in-law. They were shopping somewhere else. Kym was lying low. I'd dreaded the day she went to work for one of my competitors, but that hadn't materialized.

"Where are you going?" I asked. Freddy had been headed in the opposite direction than I was going.

"Same place as you. The chapel. For the *mandatory* meeting," he said, tugging on my arm to turn me around.

Oh, that. "Boy, I don't want to go. That woman hates me. She seems to have it out for me."

"Mercedes? Really? Everyone loves her."

"She just pulled a fake gun on a quilter's husband."

Freddy laughed. I looked at him in surprise. Laughter wasn't the reaction I'd expected.

"She likes to think she's part of the Wild West," he said. "Don't let her get under your skin. This can be a marvelous week. A magical place. You'll learn more here than you would in a year at your quilt shop."

I tried to process what he was saying. I'd had an inkling of that in class today, and remembered now how stoked I'd felt.

Freddy caught my upper arm. "I'll protect you, babe." He grinned like the Big Bad Wolf.

I was spared a more intimate view of his orthodonture as he turned when his name was called.

"Freddy, wait up," someone called. We turned to see a fair-haired man, dressed in a blue-striped shirt with white collar and red suspenders, climbing the steps and waving.

"Quentin, you made it," Freddy said gleefully. "I thought you weren't going to get here."

"My flight was delayed until this morning," he said. "I went straight to my class."

"I was afraid I was going to be the only male at the seminar," Freddy said insincerely.

"That would have been tragic," I teased. "All these women and only you to flirt with."

"He still has the corner on that market," the new guy said. "I don't flirt with your kind."

Freddy and Quentin shook hands. The pair couldn't have been more different. Quentin's tan khakis were neatly pressed and he wore matching suede Hush Puppies, a shoe Freddy wouldn't have traded in his

Ferragamos for on a bet. His hair was thinning on top, leaving him with a fringe of sandy curls. His face was ruddy, which might have been the exertion of the long staircase built into the hillside.

They obviously liked one another. Maybe it was because they were males in a mostly feminine world. They were probably thrown together at most events.

Quentin drew back and looked Freddy up and down. "Why is it you dress more gay than I do? You attract women with that style?"

"Only women of impeccable taste." Freddy did the honors. "Dewey Pellicano, meet Quentin Rousseau, of New Orleans."

Freddy tried to pronounce New Orleans like a native, slurring, but judging by Quentin's wince, he missed by a mile.

Quentin held out his hand and I shook his meaty hand. He gave me a shy smile, revealing deep dimples. I was feeling a little more disposed to like him.

"Quentin is the premier longarm quilter in the South. He specializes in quilting whole cloths with fancy-schmancy designs," Freddy told me.

"Mercedes must be thrilled you're here," Freddy said, his hand clasping Quentin's elbow. "You know how she hates to have her count off."

"God forbid, there should be nineteen people in class," he said, with a soft, gentle cadence. He didn't have a thick Southern accent, but his words had a languidness to them that spoke of long, hot summer days. "Ruins her feng shui. She's got a thing about round numbers."

I remembered the conversations about the missing quilter that I'd heard at breakfast. "What about the Ghost? Do you know about her?"

Quentin and Freddy exchanged a smirk and laughed. "So you heard about the so-called Ghost?" Freddy said. "I'm surprised you fell for that."

"It's not true?" I asked. I swallowed my next words quickly. I'd been just about to tell him about the woman screaming in the night.

Freddy shrugged. "She's never been missing from one of my classes. I've been teaching here for five years."

I looked at Quentin. He shook his head. "Never had the pleasure."

Freddy said, "Dewey here has already incurred the wrath of Mercedes. She even pulled her Annie Oakley routine on her."

He laughed. Quentin said, "Don't worry, hon, her bark is worse than her bite. I'll tell you who I'm dying to meet. Mercedes has a new assistant."

Quentin and Freddy had a love of gossip in common. Freddy leaned in while Quentin continued.

"Oh dear, a new Mini-Mer? If you're interested in ghosts, Dewey, maybe you ought to look into what happened to all of the old assistants. We meet a new one just about every year. We've learned not to get too attached. One minute they're here and the next, poof! They're gone. Mercedes cannot hold on to her help," Quentin said.

"So true, my man," Freddy said, "If I want to keep my job, and I do, I'd better get inside."

Quentin rubbed his meaty hands together. "I heard there's a display of antique sewing implements," he said.

"I'm not sure I want to go," I said. I still hadn't made up my mind about staying.

"Come on, you know you want to know what an ear wax spoon is for," Freddy said.

"A what?" I asked. "Gross."

Freddy hooked an arm through mine again. "Let's go."

The chapel was a glorious example of Craftsman-style architecture, so of course, my heart beat a little faster when Quentin opened the door and indicated I should go in first. The ceiling beams soared overhead, reminiscent of the cathedral-like atmosphere created naturally by old-growth trees deep in the forest. Sconces lit the room. Built-in chairs, their seats folded up, were in straight rows on the slanted floor facing the stage and the huge window that looked over the dunes outside. There were two sets of curtains. The first was tied back at the edge of the proscenium and the second, when closed, would cover the window beyond.

Nan Orchard was at the front of the room, talking to Mercedes and being fitted for a wireless mike. She tested the sound with a breathy, one, two, three.

People were milling about the room, their voices echoing in the space. Along the northern side of the building was an alcove anchored by a stone fireplace, with built-in woodboxes on either side. When the crowd moved, I could see tables set up in there. Quilters were lined up, looking at the display of antique sewing tools and boxes.

We got closer. I wasn't expecting the beauty that was arranged on the tabletop. The sewing boxes were striking, with elaborate decoration. There were a dozen or more, ranging in size from a jewelry box size up to a bread box. They were made of wood, tin, and enamel. I recognized marquetry, inlaid wood designs, and cloisonné enamel work. These boxes might be utilitarian, but each one was a work of art.

Beauty, form, and function, the trifecta of the Arts and Crafts Movement. Julia Morgan, the architect, would love these.

Freddy said, "I'll plop my stuff down, save us some seats."

"Get us as close as you can to the stage," Quentin said, pointing a long finger. "I want to hear her talk."

Freddy walked away. Quentin and I looked over the sewing tool display. I had no idea what most of these things were. My sewing tools consisted of a sewing machine, often an iron and fusing medium. These tools, meant to be used for hand sewing and darning, had no context for me.

Finally, I recognized something. I stopped in front of a board full of neck chains.

"My mother wore one of these," I said, reading the sign that identified them as chatelaines. "I didn't know that's what they were called."

These chatelaines were like jewelry. The chain was worn around the neck, with a suspended pocket that could hold a needle and a pair of scissors. My mother had made them out of cloth, decorated with pins and buttons and lace.

The memory was a dim one, but I remember my mother staying up late one night, making matching chatelaines for all her workers, the night before a big sale at the shop. I was about twelve. I'd helped, picking out the lace to decorate the cloth and tying scissors to ribbons that she'd sewed on. Ina probably still had hers, although I couldn't recall her wearing it lately. I wondered where my mother's was.

Probably in the sewing room that had once been the boys' bedroom. My father had closed that door when she died. None of us had had the heart to open it since. I had to think about getting some of her friends together to clean it out soon.

Quentin had stopped in front of an open sewing box made of some kind of exotic wood. He pushed an invisible button on the side, and a silk-lined drawer slid out. It contained slots for needles. I was amazed at the practical, but beautiful, workmanship.

The top tier had been taken out of the main box and laid alongside. It was a tray that was fitted with spaces for sewing tools, the shape of each one clearly outlined. Every tool had its own compartment in the velvet tray. The box was lined in red silk, tufted with ivory buttons.

I began to see the potential in these boxes.

I wondered if any were for sale. I had a few customers who might be interested.

"This box is made of bones," Quentin whispered. "Bones."

A shiver ran down my back. "Whose bones?"

Freddy joined us. "Those are the bones of machine quilters hung in the great Singer uprising of 1888."

I laughed. Freddy was fun to have around. Quentin rubbed a finger along the edge of the table, clearly holding himself back from touching the tools.

Nan Williams came up behind us. "Prisoners made them out of soup bones. Look at the workmanship. Have you ever seen anything like that?"

I could honestly say I hadn't. The tools were highly polished, each one seated in its own place.

"I don't know what half of this stuff is used for," I admitted. "But I am intrigued."

Nan pointed to a small squat spool, half the size of a normal thread. "Those are bobbins. The ladies would take the thread off the spool and wind it on those. Those are made of ivory." She pointed to another utensil. "That's a tweezers."

That one I did recognize. I stepped away from the bone box, and pointed to another that looked like tiny inlaid tiles. "What about this one?"

"From India," she said. "They liked to do that intricate tile work."

The next exhibit was a wooden marquetry box. The sign said it was made from mahogany and zebrawood. The finish on the wood shone and caught the light from the sconces overhead. It looked like it would feel hot to the touch.

Nan said, "A woman's sewing box was her treasure. A status symbol. Historically, sewing was becoming a choice and not a chore, and these boxes became popular. The lady of the house always had mending to do."

"What about servants? Wouldn't women like that have servants?"

Quentin's face clouded over. "They used the boxes, but didn't own them. It always belonged to the lady of the house."

I guessed poor Quentin had relatives who'd been exploited. "Are they valuable?" I asked.

Nan had moved on to answer a question, so it was Quentin who responded. "Can be. There's been a resurgence in interest since eBay has made it easier to collect them. If the kit has good provenance it could be extremely valuable."

"Are you a collector?" I asked.

Freddy wedged himself between the two of us. "Quentin is a first-class dabbler. He has a button collection, a cigar-band collection, and the most silk ties of any man on either side of the Mississippi."

Quentin didn't hear his teasing. He'd stopped in front of a sewing box made of rosewood, the grain of the wood visible. The blue velvet tray was clearly missing one of the tools, but that didn't stop Quentin from staring.

The aisle was getting crowded. I felt someone jostle my back. I was ready to sit down. The number of people brushing against me was getting uncomfortable.

Freddy read the card on the box Quentin had stopped in front of. "The Rose Box. Thought to be from the property of the young queen of France."

"Too bad it's not complete," I said.

"The sewing bird," Quentin said. He pointed to a space in the top tray. The shape of the tool was clearly visible. It looked like a bird on a stick with a clamp on the bottom.

"What's it used for?" I asked.

"You could call it a third hand. You screwed it to the tabletop. The bird's mouth opened and gripped the fabric you were sewing," Quentin said.

I tried to picture it, but couldn't really see how it worked. My hand mending experience was nonexistent.

"What was it made of?" I asked.

"Most were metal. Some were fancy with filigree work. This one looks pretty straight-forward."

He traced the shape of it.

We caught up again to Nan, who was ahead of us, pointing out the most unique features of the tools and boxes.

She said, "Ear wax was used to strengthen thread along with beeswax. It was more readily available, that's for sure. The spoons were used to obtain the substance."

"Told you," Freddy said.

Ewww. I thought about the antique quilts I'd seen. How many of them had been quilted with earwax? I rubbed my hands on my jeans.

"Why aren't these things in a museum?" I asked. "I mean, the quilt museum in San Jose should want this stuff."

Nan shook her head. "Our quilt museums are woefully underfunded. They don't have room to store everything they're offered. The staff has to make serious choices about what they can take in. In fact, some of these kits came from the New England Quilt Museum who sold off some of their artifacts to raise funds."

"That's a shame," I said. It would be nice if more people could get a look at these pieces.

A shout was heard from the other end of the display. Nan looked up, startled. She absently handed a heavily beaded scissor fob to Quentin, who was standing next to her. He laid it down quickly into the slotted space that was made for it. Freddy craned his neck to see what was going on.

A crowd had gathered around one of the tables. We followed Nan.

"This is an outrage," I heard someone say. It sounded like Harriet, the New Yorker, who had been in my class.

She held up a sewing box lid over her head as though she was going to dash it into the fireplace. Nan gasped. Freddy leapt forward to steady the woman's hand. She angrily pulled away from him.

"Look at that, people." Harriet held the lid up higher so everyone could see. She pointed to the inlaid wood design that decorated the lid. "Just look and tell me you're not as appalled as I am."

She turned the lid so everyone could see. "Right there. It's a swastika."

Six

The crowd took a step back as if we were line dancing at the Saddlerack. Nan stepped forward and gingerly took the lid from the woman's hand. Her ample bosom was heaving.

"Those are German crosses, Harriet," she said. "Not swastikas. Just because Hitler used a similar motif for his evil doesn't mean everything with that design is suspect."

"You shouldn't have brought it here," Harriet said, her face dimpling with red spots. "No one wants to see that."

Nan's voice was shaking. "This is a piece that is over a hundred years old. Well before World War II was fought. There is no reason it has to hide away, shamefaced because of what the Nazis did. This has nothing to do with Nazis."

"People don't know that," Harriet said. Her eyes were shiny with tears.

Nan's chest was puffed out like a pigeon's. "Then people should be educated."

Mercedes appeared and stepped between the two women. Harriet was not backing down. She and Nan were staring at one another. I looked to see if Mercedes was armed this time, too. Thankfully, there was no gun in sight.

"Let's take a breath, please," Mercedes said. She took the lid from Harriet's hand and placed it back on the box, moving the box away from the edge of the table, but keeping one hand on it.

Harriet's eyes flashed.

Mercedes said, "This is art, Harriet. Art has no politics. Let's take our seats."

Mercedes pushed people toward the rows of seats. Harriet threw up her arms and walked out.

Freddy led the way to where he'd laid his yellow coat across three chairs in the third row back. We sat down. I looked back and saw Lucy take a seat, reluctantly, it appeared. She had not gone out with Harriet.

Mercedes waited for the crowd to quiet. Nan took her place on the stage. I recognized the ranger who joined her.

"Before we get started, there have been some questions about the animals you might encounter. This is Ranger Tony Pelli-

78

cano," Mercedes said. "He'll fill us in."

Freddy turned to me, eyebrow cocked in question.

Quentin said, "A relation?"

I beamed. "My brother."

Tony stepped up to the podium, nodding at Mercedes. He held his hat in his hand, turning it as he talked, the only sign that he was even a little bit nervous.

"You may have noticed some fawns in the park."

He was interrupted by oohs and aahs from the crowd. They were ready to leave Harriet's hysteria behind.

"Yes, they're adorable," Tony said. The word adorable didn't seem right coming out of my brother's mouth. I stifled a giggle.

"Talk about adorable," the quilter in front of me whispered. "He can lay his hat on my bed any ole time."

"I bet he's really good with his hands," her friend whispered back. "Gentle."

"But firm," her friend countered. The two had their heads together.

Freddy elbowed me, laughing. I shushed him, and the quilters, too, I hoped, by proxy. I was getting embarrassed for Tony.

"I know you've heard about our mountain lion." Tony continued. "She has been known to frequent the area this time of year. You'll need to take precautions, especially at dawn and dusk. The lion is nocturnal, so chances are you won't see her. But I hear you quilters like to be up rather late . . ." He waited for a laugh but none came.

Tony's joke fell flat, and I winced for him. He didn't have our father's natural way with women. Too many years in the woods.

A quilter raised her hand and Tony acknowledged her question.

"Isn't it true that mountain lions only attack if they're sick or in pain?" she asked.

"Some people believe that," he said, his eyes returning to his notes. It was obvious that he did not concur. "Just in case, don't walk quietly. Talk loudly," Tony continued.

"That explains why no quilters have ever been attacked," Freddy stage-whispered. "They never shut up long enough for the lion to get near."

"If you see a mountain lion, do this," Tony said, raising his arms over his head. "Don't run away: make yourself as large as you can. Do not, I repeat, do *not* bend over."

"Most of these people haven't bent over since Clinton was president," Freddy said. He was on a roll.

"And never turn your back on the lion."

"Just like most of my boyfriends," Quentin snarked.

Tony finished up. "Call a ranger if you have any questions. There are house phones on all of the buildings. Just dial the number on the card. If you follow these steps, I'm sure you'll have a wonderful time here at Asilomar."

Polite clapping followed Tony as he left the stage.

Nan gave her lecture about the history of sewing boxes. Her passion, that had been so evident earlier, didn't come across in her talk — she'd obviously been shaken by Harriet's outburst.

After dinner, I tried to get Vangie, but she'd gone home. The pay phone was in use. I couldn't reach Buster and I missed him. I could have gone back to the sewing room with my class, but I was tired of sewing. I found a paperback on the communal shelf in the Administration building and went to my room.

Finally, I went to bed, dreaming about Nazis and mountain lions.

Seven

Tuesday morning, I woke up early. I felt an unease I couldn't explain. Maybe it was the tail end of a dream. I knew part of it was not being home in my own bed, being cut off from Vangie and the store, and part of it was missing Buster. And Tony's talk about mountain lions had not helped. I did not want to run into one of those cats.

I wondered if I'd been awakened by a noise. I listened again. The fog was softening sounds. I glanced at the plastic alarm clock on the bedside table. Tony's nature walk was scheduled in a few minutes. If I hurried, I'd make it. I took a quick shower and pulled on jeans and a sweatshirt.

I wanted to find out where he'd been yesterday. He'd missed our coffee date, and then disappeared before Nan's lecture was over. I couldn't imagine that a lot of quilters would be up at this hour.

Darn. I was wrong. At least a dozen

women were scattered on the steps of the social hall. Tony was on the top step, looking crisp and wide awake in his two-tone ranger uniform. He'd begun his talk already.

"Your sewing seminar is in the tradition of Asilomar's role as a women's retreat. Architect Julia Morgan designed sixteen buildings, thirteen of which still remain. The buildings are in the Arts and Crafts style, which emphasizes raw materials and utilizes the site's natural attributes."

He'd done his homework since yesterday. I gave him a quick smile.

Tony pointed out the features of the building behind him and the dining hall. Both featured stone pillars and redwood siding. Being an Arts and Crafts geek, I'd read everything I could about the architecture before I came down, so I tuned out. I saw no familiar faces in the crowd of quilters. No one to buddy up with.

The group moved slowly through the circle that Julia Morgan had designed as the axis for all the buildings.

I took another look at the buildings behind us. In the center, the administration building, to the right, the dining hall, and over to the left, the chapel. Perfection.

Asilomar looked so different without the bright sunshine that had prevailed yesterday.

Fog had settled in today, not too thick, just enough to give me a feeling like my eyes were draped in gauze. I couldn't see beyond the first line of dunes. The trees looked austere.

"Let's head to the beach," Tony said.

Tony herded the group of women toward the boardwalk, talking all the while. The quilters were uncharacteristically quiet.

"The planking material is a recycled plastic and the boardwalk travels through the most delicate ecosystem in the park. These dunes are ever changing. Plants are getting a foothold again. You'll see the endangered Tidestrom's Lupine. The beach sage has become one of our anchor plants."

I caught up to the group midway up the boardwalk. The ocean was visible, looking cold, a mist gathering on the surface. All the paths around Asilomar were designed for maximum surprises. They twisted and turned so that the pedestrian was always challenged by the view.

Since I couldn't talk to him, I decided to give Tony a tough time. He was being adored by the middle-aged women surrounding him, and I couldn't let him rest on his laurels. Good-natured razzing was a long-standing Pellicano tradition.

"Is it true that the YWCA girls used the

dunes as their sports arena?" I asked.

Tony caught sight of me. He frowned, and only the presence of his hat stopped him from scratching his head. "Perhaps," he said carefully. "But Asilomar is doing all it can to preserve the natural habitat. The dunes are home to many small species of insects."

Tony droned on about worms. I listened, waiting for my next opportunity to heckle him.

We reached the road. It was crosshatched with a pedestrian walkway, but drivers could be distracted by the great expanse of beautiful blue ocean out their windows. Or the antics of surfers in the crashing waves. Tony looked carefully both ways, then led us across.

The berm was crowded with parked cars. Surfers sat on the side of the road, talking quietly, waiting for the sky to illuminate the surf enough to make it safe to get out there. Right now the waves looked gentle. Only two souls could be seen paddling out.

To the south, the beach curved gracefully, forming a protective cove before going out to Point Joe. The waves lowered there, making it a good place to catch a wave.

Tony waited for an older woman in bright pink pants to catch up. He pointed to the white-sand beach under our feet. "We like to call the sand squeaky clean. Try it. Scrape your feet along the sand and see if you can make it sing."

The half-dozen women obliged. Tony shot me a look that made me rub my feet, too. I grinned at him. It was fun to watch him in charge but this was an easy audience. Most of these women were just excited to be around a man. A good-looking guy like Tony in a uniform with a loaded gun was almost too much for some of them to bear.

Tony continued, raising his voice to be heard over the roar of the ocean, "The sand consists only of broken-up quartz which accounts for its pristine, white appearance."

I dutifully raised my hand. In my most concerned voice, I said, "Have you ever *seen* a mountain lion?"

Tony frowned. Several of the quilters nudged each other. "No, I have not."

"How do you know there's one around here?" I asked.

"We can tell she's in the area because of the signs she leaves behind. She scratches on trees to mark her territory. She leaves behind scat."

"Scat?" The woman next to me said.

"Poop," I filled in.

Tony gave me another glare. "Let's move on to the tidal pools. They're fascinating.

Many, many animals live just below the surface of the water."

He moved the group back onto the road. We walked slowly north, then veered onto a path that ran parallel to the ocean. We were well back from the water's edge. The path meandered through the sand and high dunes. Rock croppings came in and out, forming tide pools. The tide was still coming in, so many rocks were visible.

I grew impatient — the group was not going fast enough for me. I took off down the path. I was working up a sweat, despite the cool air, when I saw a pile of dog crap on the side of the path. I looked back to see where Tony and his group were. The path had curved in a way that I could see golfers a half-mile away on Spanish Bay Golf Course, but I couldn't see Tony, who was much closer.

I toyed with the idea of yelling that I'd found mountain lion scat.

I decided not to. I was enjoying my alone time. I continued to move quickly and put some distance between myself and the group. Tony's voice came and then faded. I jogged a little.

The surf grew higher. Storms offshore had whipped up the waves. Rain was predicted for later. Action felt good. I felt myself waking up, my muscles coming alive and begging for more. The cobwebs started to lift from my brain.

A knocking noise startled me, and I looked around for the source. There was no other person in sight. I heard it again, and turned my head. Out in the shallow water of the cove, a sea otter was lying on its back, bouncing an abalone shell on a rock lying on its chest, getting ready to feast.

I felt my heart rate return to normal. Buster was right. He'd told me I'd been living in the city too long, away from nature. I had to get used to the noises that were a normal part of life in the wild — not sirens, or kids skateboarding by. I wondered if he and I could spend more time down here. A few hikes, maybe even a scuba trip would help me get back to Mother Earth.

I climbed a rock, looking out to sea. The expanse of the Pacific was overwhelming. I sighed. Too bad Buster wasn't here to share it with me. I felt lonely in this view of emptiness.

I looked back, but couldn't see Tony. I climbed over the rocks, feeling their slippery surfaces, and moved carefully back onto the designated route, still moving away from Tony and the quilters.

A couple of hundred yards ahead of me,

the path was closed for construction, orange cones and caution tape forbidding egress. I stopped, trying to figure out where to go next.

Below me, the rocks made a precarious walkway. The fog was affecting my field of vision. I could see a couple of hundred yards ahead of me, but no further, so I moved back toward the road.

An old Volkswagen van was parked in the sandy shoulder. When I was in college back east, my new roommate had asked me what kind of bus my family drove. In New Jersey where she was from, everyone assumed all Californians surfed and drove old beat-up VWs. While singing Partridge Family songs in harmony, no doubt.

The tune of "Muskrat Love" came to me. Damn Buster anyhow for giving me an ear-worm.

Ahead of me was a larger outcropping that jutted out into the ocean. A sign read, "Since 1968, forty-five people have been swept out to sea. The waters here are dangerous and changeable. Use extreme caution. Stay on the path."

But I'd lost the path. Then the fog lifted a little, and ahead of me I saw something.

Someone had disobeyed the sign. A lone figure stood on the edge of a high rock.

Hard to tell for sure, but it looked like a woman, her long red curls whipped straight out behind her. She stood on the edge, arms spread Titanic-like, as though she was playing queen of the world. She was wearing a patchwork cape, made from what looked like silks and velvets, like a crazy quilt.

Those fabrics would be ruined by the salty spray. I yelled at her to get back. I took several steps toward her.

I moved around a pile of rocks, and suddenly I saw her again. As the wind whipped through her hair, I was reminded of the cypress in the park a few miles along, their odd asymmetrical growth pushed by wind and shaped into strange sculptures that bore little resemblance to trees.

This was one place where you could see the wind, or at least the results of its force.

The woman wasn't looking at me. She was very close to the edge. My heart stopped for a moment as a loose rock skittered from under her foot and fell the twenty feet to the ocean below, then was lost in the foam.

"Be careful," I called, unable to stop myself. She looked so ethereal, so otherworldly — I didn't know if she could hear me or if she knew how close she was to the edge.

The cliffs were not high here, but the

water was cold and deep. I knew the water off the Monterey coast was ten thousand feet deep in places — dark cold waters where strange creatures lived and giant kelp forests grew. Not good for human survival.

"Move away from the edge," I called, feeling the winds whip my words away. She gave no sign of hearing me.

I walked slowly, not wanting to startle the woman and have her trip and perhaps fall from the rocks because of my voice. I couldn't be responsible for this woman's life. Or death.

Time slowed, as I pushed my foot in front of myself, scattering rocks in front of me. I froze. The noise I made seemed so loud to me. I was sure I'd given her reason to start. But she was still standing, watching the horizon line, as if looking for answers on the high seas. Facing the emptiness. The void.

The rocks around her were wet, despite their height above the shore. Waves could, and did, wash up this far. People were always drowning, dragged out to sea by rogue waves and wicked under-currents.

"Miss? Hello?" I yelled. "Can you hear me?"

Where were Tony and the quilters? I looked back where the path had been, but couldn't see them. I called for him, but I didn't want to take my eyes off the woman in front of me, so my call was snatched away by the wind.

She turned. Her skin was pale, and I wondered if she was from another time or place. Or if I was imagining her. I blinked, but she was still there. A large wave hit the rock, the spray scattering majestically. She had to be getting wet, but she didn't flinch. The idea of permanent water stains on her cape made me sick.

I was approaching the woman now, but she turned back to the surf, completely absorbed in the sight of the sea crashing into the rocks.

I looked back to see if Tony was behind me yet. I yelled for him again, but there was no answer.

I turned back to the woman on the rock.

But she was gone. I looked up to the road, expecting to see her striding away. No one was there. She had disappeared.

That was ridiculous. I had looked away for a moment. There was no one else around. I hadn't heard anything, just the relentless motion of the waves crashing against the rocks, and being sucked back out again.

Where did she go? My heart beat wildly.

She hadn't had enough time to get to the roadway, and I had a clear view of the path ahead. I waited to see if she appeared further along the path, but there was nothing.

My heart leapt into my throat. What if she'd gone over the edge? A wave might have pulled her in, joining the ranks of so many others. John Denver had gone down in his plane not far from here, and I remembered reading about a honeymooning couple swept off a rock at Lovers' Point. Waves were unpredictable.

I walked past the rope, feeling a little like the time I'd crossed the yellow tape of a crime scene.

On the rocks below was the cape of many colors, spread-eagled, the red lining like a gash.

EIGHT

I glanced around. No one was visible on the path. Tony and the quilters were somewhere behind me. I took a step toward the street. The road was empty. The surfers I'd seen earlier were a half mile up the beach, protected in the cove. Even if one happened to look up right now, there was no way anyone could come help me.

She was gone. Nothing. I scrambled down the rocks, grabbing a weed for a hold. My hand slid off and I fell on my butt, digging my heels in to stop my downward slide. I sat there. It would do her no good if I went in after her. People died on the coast all the time trying to save their companions.

I pushed myself backward to the relative safety of the sandy ground, and lay there, panting. My breath was coming in waves, my stomach roiled as though it wanted to give up its contents.

I looked into the sun, veiled behind a

curtain of fog, blinking away the spots that appeared in front of my eyes. I tried to comprehend the vast open space where once the woman had stood in front of me. How had that happened?

The ocean had swallowed her, with not so much as a burp. She was nothing to the vast expanse of water. The tide continued its path, in and out. I shivered, feeling suddenly lonely again. A cloud crossed in front of the sun. The wind picked up.

The gloom I'd felt this morning returned. I'd seen more dead bodies than most people. Had I woken up somehow knowing what lay ahead for me today? I needed to stand, but felt my knees buckle. The last thing I wanted was to know the future, especially when it involved dying.

I reached for my phone. Of course, it was not on my hip.

The sound of a car got me to my feet. I ran to the road. A VW bus passed me slowly, rumbling by, gears grinding, shrieking as it maneuvered the slight rise. I waved at the driver, trying to get her to slow, to pick me up, but she didn't see me, and the van just continued its laboring ascent, still moving faster than I was.

There was no sign of Tony and his crew. I didn't realize how far ahead of them I'd gotten. I raced back toward them, toward Asilomar, toward help.

Finally, I heard Tony and saw him on his haunches pointing into a tidal pool. I called to him. He stood, and excused himself from the group.

"Tony!" I stopped, trying to catch my breath. A sudden stitch in my side caused every gasp to cut me. I gulped.

"Come with me," I got out, letting my hand slip into his palm and pulling on it. I felt instantly calmer. This was my big brother. Holding his hand, showing him something, was a familiar, visceral action, taking me right back to my childhood. Except instead of a broken robin's egg on the sidewalk, I was showing him where someone had died.

"I saw a woman fall into the ocean," I said, whispering. I didn't want the quilters to hear me. There was no point in ruining their day, too.

Tony understood, and turned to his tour group. "Sorry, folks. I've got to cut our time short. It's been a pleasure talking to you."

He tipped his hat and we took off down the path.

"When? Where?" Tony was moving quickly now.

I thought about how long it had taken me

to run back here. Too long. The ocean was cold. "Probably ten minutes ago."

"Was she struggling? Did you see her break the surface?"

"No," I said. "One minute she was on the cliff, the next minute she was gone."

Tony stopped, waiting for me to catch up. I was breathing like the Niles Canyon Railroad. "You never saw her again?" Tony said. His eyes, looking out on the water, were troubled.

I shook my head, seeing on his face that it was hopeless.

Tony turned away and spoke into his walkie-talkie. "I've got a witness who saw a person go into the ocean."

He waited for an answer, then gave our location. "I'm headed there now."

He turned to me. "Show me."

His gait slowed, and the urgency had gone out of his voice. This was not a matter of life and death anymore.

I showed him the cape. It had floated out to a rock, the water flowing over it shifting the fabric, making it look like it was alive.

"That's hers," I said.

Tony climbed down nimbly, so unlike my earlier stumbling. I reminded myself this was his job. He was good at it, focused and strong. I felt a wave of pride.

He stood looking out to sea, then fished the cape out of the water.

Within minutes, we were joined by the Lifeguard Rangers, the Coast Guard, trucks from the local fire department. The Pacific Grove Police and Monterey County Sheriff's Department cars lined the roadway. Talking quietly, the group divided duties. Tony joined the rangers in roping off the area. Lifeguards in wet suits went into the water where the woman had disappeared. A boat offshore launched a small craft. A helicopter came over the horizon.

The bustle of activity left me drained, and I leaned against a rail fence. The other quilters had decided to go back to Asilomar and wait for news, but the police wanted to talk to me.

Tony found me. I could feel my lower lip trembling but was unable to stop it. "Are you cold?" he asked.

I nodded. Feeling cold was easier than what I was really feeling — dread.

Tony fetched a blanket from a patrol car and offered it to me, wrapping me like a burrito. He gave an extra tug, bringing the material around my neck.

"Sorry," he said. "These things take time."

I knew that. Tony had been away while I'd solved two murders in the last year. We'd never really discussed my role. I let him think I was the innocent baby sister he'd left behind. I was okay with that.

"Did she fall, Dewey?" Tony asked. I shook my head. "Lose her footing?"

"I don't know," I wailed. I felt a welling of sadness fill my chest. "She was there one minute, gone the next."

"She took off her cape," he said.

I nodded, not wanting to acknowledge what he was saying.

"It had to be deliberate," Tony said thoughtfully.

I closed my eyes. I tried, but I couldn't think of an alternate scenario. Whoever this woman was, she'd decided to end her life in the Pacific Ocean. How awful.

Tony put a protective arm around me, and squeezed. "I'm sorry you had to see that, sis. I've seen more than my share of suicides. They're always an inexplicable waste."

"Can I take your statement?" A Pacific Grove cop approached us. He was a middle-aged man with a deep tan that I'd bet didn't extend past his collar. Right now, his face was creased with worry.

"Detective Graham," he introduced himself. "Let's walk back the way you came."

A crowd was gathering at the edge of the road. Tony stopped to make sure they stayed well back. A couple of surfers, wetsuits peeled down to reveal pasty chests, and a cadre of older men watched the proceedings. One geezer was extremely excited about the helicopter, pointing and jabbing his friend with his walking stick. We walked until we were out of earshot.

I led the detective to where I'd first seen the woman. I filled him in as he took notes.

"I guess you see this a lot," I said.

He smiled kindly. "Too often to suit me," he said. His eyes slanted downward, a permanent sadness etched into his wrinkles.

I wanted to ask him the question I hadn't asked Tony. "Do you think I could have saved her?"

"No," he said softly. "If anything, she may have been waiting for a witness."

A witness? The thought chilled me. Why me? The words almost escaped my lips but I choked them back. I knew there was no good answer.

"Is it okay if I go back to Asilomar?" I asked. "I'm staying there for a conference."

"Sure," he said. "Best thing you can do is return to your routine. We'll handle things out here."

I was glad to be out of it. Tony could tell me what happened later. I headed back toward the gates that led to the Asilomar boardwalk. My feet felt like bricks, and my thighs burned as though I'd walked straight uphill for miles.

By the wooden Asilomar sign, I heard my name being called, and turned. The rescue effort was out of sight.

It was Paul Wiggins. "Dewey, right?" he said.

"What are you doing here?" I asked, my voice rising in fear. This was the man Mercedes had threatened with a gun yesterday. I took several steps backward and looked over my shoulder. Now I could see the edge of the fire and rescue truck. I moved further away from Paul. I wanted to be sure someone could see us.

My foot slipped on the gravel as I back-pedaled and I nearly tripped. He put out a hand to steady me. I pulled my arm away, nearly toppling over in the process.

"What do you want?" I asked.

"Still trying to get to Ursula, my wife." He seemed to be trying to sound wounded, but it was pitiful. "Mercedes has the wrong idea about us."

I doubted that. Women don't usually reveal their husbands to be batterers just for the sake of conversation.

I held up my hand. I shivered. "Sorry, I don't have time for this."

A siren sounded. Paul's eyes looked past me. "What's going on back there?"

"A woman was swept off a cliff," I said, refusing to say more than that.

Paul's expression froze. "Did you see her?" he asked me gruffly.

I nodded. Words couldn't get out of the tightness that was my chest and throat right now.

He grabbed my upper arm. "Tell me."

"Ouch," I cried. I pushed his hand away. My heart raced. I willed Tony to look my way.

Paul's face softened, although his eyes remained steely. He held his hands up and away from me. "I'm sorry, I'm just so worried about Ursula."

He reached into his coat pocket. I flinched, but he only pulled out a picture.

"Is this her?" he said, his hand trembling. I took the print from him, turning away so he couldn't see my face. I didn't want to be so exposed in front of this man.

A tall auburn-haired woman looked defiantly into the camera. Her smile was slightly crooked, the result of a broken jaw, according to Mercedes.

I felt the jolt of recognition cross my face. This was the woman I'd just seen standing on a rock in the Pacific Ocean. I glanced at

Paul, but he was looking at his wife.

"It's the last picture I took of her. She was leaving for the airport," he said.

Defiance was the last thing I'd expected to see on Ursula's face. I didn't know any battered women, but I'd expected to see a tired woman, worn out from fighting an indefatigable enemy. One that lived in her own home. In her bedroom.

Maybe Mercedes had overreacted to Paul's presence yesterday. God knows she was prone to overstatement. This woman looked proud. And hopeful.

I tried to let him down easy. "I can't be sure of what I saw," I began. I was not convincing anyone, including myself. I'd never be an actress.

He took back the picture, trying unsuccessfully to fold it into a neat package again. I could see I'd shot an arrow into his heart.

"It was her," he said. "I had a feeling she would do something like this —"

"The police, the rangers, the Coast Guard, they're all looking for her," I said. "Don't give up hope."

He crumpled the picture in his hand, clutching it so tight, his knuckles turned white. I flinched at the sight of his fist.

I wanted to be free of his oppressive presence. "Mr. Wiggins, you need to go to the police. Tell them you think it's your wife. They will keep you apprised."

He nodded, and started plodding back toward the scene. His shoulders slumped. I watched him for several moments, but he wasn't making much headway.

I turned into the Asilomar grounds. Paul called to me.

"Keep your eyes and ears open back at Asilomar. This has something to do with Sewing-by-the-Sea. I know it."

I shook off his parting shot. He was almost right. I was the reason Ursula had leapt into the ocean. She was trying to escape from her predator, her husband. The man I'd brought onto the grounds.

NINE

Ursula had killed herself because her husband had nearly found her. She had to realize that there was no escaping him.

How had she found out about Paul's visit to Asilomar?

There was only one way that Ursula could have found out that Paul was here. Mercedes. I had to find her and get to the bottom of things.

Breakfast was over. I looked into the empty dining hall but there was no sign of Mercedes. I couldn't believe it was only 9:30 a.m. So much was going on, just down the road a mile or so, out of sight.

I strode past the dining hall and up the hill past Merrill Hall, its majestic façade like a stone ship rising from the earth.

All of the residence halls at Asilomar were designed with a common room on the first floor. Many of these rooms were dominated by a fireplace, and most had a piano. These rooms were left unlocked around the clock so that visitors could enjoy all aspects of Asilomar.

Mercedes was using the living room of the Pirates' Den as an office. The building had two public bathrooms off the living room, and five sleeping rooms. The land sloped behind the building, so the back half also had a lower level, which housed another private room.

I could see Mercedes sitting at a pine table set under the window on top of a vein-patterned green carpet. Two chairs with burnished leather seats and padded arms were pulled away from the wall. Papers were spread out on the table. I was glad the orange curtains were closed against the view of pine trees, feeding deer, and the ocean in the distance. Too pretty for this discussion.

As I entered, the bathroom door swung closed. I heard the water running as I walked into the room.

"Mercedes, a woman fell into the ocean," I said.

Mercedes looked up from her paperwork, unfocused, her finger holding her place on the spreadsheet she had in front of her. She obviously did not comprehend what I'd said.

"That's too bad," she said and went back

to her work.

"Mercedes," I said. "I think you know her."

She tilted her head. "Was it one of my students?"

"It's worse than that," I said. "Paul Wiggins thinks it might be his wife, Ursula. Did you tell her he was here?"

Mercedes' gaze unfocused, her pencil eraser tapping her bright white teeth again and again. She was leaving little pink bits behind. Her orthodontist would not approve.

"Ursula? No way. I told you two yesterday that she's not attending the conference this year. She didn't sign up."

"Well, she was here. She threw herself off a rock a half mile from where we are standing," I said.

Mercedes pointed her pencil at me. She tapped the pages in front of her. "I don't know anything about that. She's not a part of the conference."

"The police will want to talk to you."

She shook her head. "I've got my hands full. I'm dealing with a kosher student's meals and an asthmatic complaining about the tree pollen. A diabetic who's misplaced her insulin." She shook her files at me. "I'll talk to them if they come, but I've got a lot of immediate concerns. A former student is not one of them."

A fat raccoon trundled by the open door and I shivered.

An extremely short, and mostly round, woman burst through the opening. Her generous chest was heaving and her cheeks were mottled.

Mercedes stood up. "Concordia, please take a breath. You'll hyperventilate and pass out." *Again,* she muttered under her breath.

Concordia made a beeline to Mercedes, stepping on my toe without acknowledging my presence. I stumbled out of the way. The pain was intense.

"You're doing this on purpose. My classroom is freezing. Last year it was too hot. You must come to my room and correct the situation. Now."

I recognized Concordia Filleto as an international quilting teacher, known for her unreasonableness. The internet group of shop owners I belonged to talked about her long lists of requests — no, demands — including a golf date for her husband, a cooler full of iced Diet Lemon Coke, a supply of no-longer manufactured flower-headed straight pins, a design wall of certain proportions, and an aide to help her show off her quilts.

Mercedes looked at me. It was obvious she was going to have her hands full for awhile. "I suggest you get your butt back to your class, Dewey. You've paid for it, now go. Let the police do their work."

"But Ursula?" I said. Concordia's head whipped my way when I said her name. She glanced back at Mercedes.

"Paul Wiggins is a psychopath, Dewey. You'd do well to stay out of his way. Every word he speaks is a lie. Remember that," Mercedes said. Concordia seemed to agree.

I went out of the building.

The police and Coast Guard were doing their thing. Getting in their way was not an option. I would wait until after lunch to go to class. I didn't want to disrupt the teaching and I was sure I wouldn't be able to concentrate very well. I needed to talk to someone from my real life.

I'd call the store, using our video-conferencing set up. I'd like to talk to Buster, but didn't want to give Mercedes an excuse to be mad at me. I'd try him later.

I took my laptop into the administration building and set myself up at a wooden table. I'd be talking out loud right in the middle of the room that bustled with people coming and going, but it couldn't be helped. I felt self-conscious but was desperate to touch base.

Luckily, Vangie was at her computer and answered my signal. She batted away a curl that had wandered onto her cheek.

She smiled and pulled a funny face when she saw me. "Hey, girlfriend."

The sight of her grin lifted my spirits. She and I had been through a lot in the past year, and the adversity had made us closer. She was the first one, after Buster, to whom I told all my troubles.

But we'd had a tiff just before I'd left for Asilomar. She hadn't approved of my choice of class here at the seminar: Legendary Quilts. The class had appealed to me because I knew I could manage it. A lot of the offerings here were geared to the experienced quilter. I wasn't good enough to tackle anything too complex. My quilt-making skills were severely limited. Vangie knew that, but she thought I was dogging it here. Wasting my time. I had to make sure that didn't happen.

She'd finally conceded that my coming might bring us new customers. There were three hundred quilters here, after all. She'd made sure I had plenty of business cards.

"How is Legendary Quilts going?" she'd asked. Even through the screen, I could see her eyes flashing.

"Great. Cinnamon is an amazing teacher."

"Cinnamon?" Vangie said. "Her parents named her after a spice?"

"I guess she's lucky she's not Turmeric," I said.

"Marjoram," Vangie countered. " 'Hello, my name is Marjoram. Marjoram I am.' "

I laughed as Vangie babbled, Dr. Suess style. She always knew how to brighten my day.

"So what's it like there?" she asked.

Hmmm . . . no cell phone, my car keys in lockup, the negative comments at breakfast about QP, a woman flying off the rocks into the ocean. I didn't really want to talk about what was going on here.

"How are things there?" I asked.

She looked away.

"Tell me," I said.

Vangie cracked the knuckle on her thumb and took a sip from her water bottle. I waited, my stomach knotting. This couldn't be good.

"The new hire brought her five-year-old to work yesterday. And her knitting."

My heart sunk. "Did you fire her?"

"I thought I'd leave that for you. As sucky as she is, I need the body until you get back."

Vangie and I had been unlucky when it

111

came to replacing Kym at the store. People quit after several weeks or were just plain lazy when they realized it was not fun and games. We had to fire one who did nothing but talk all day. The customers couldn't get a word in.

I tried to put on a happy face. "Who knows? Maybe that's the real reason I'm here. I'll meet someone here who's perfect to fill Kym's shoes."

"Size six, Dooney & Burke?" Vangie laughed. "With glitter toes and a handmade bow?"

Our conversation was interrupted by a bell ringing loudly. The girl behind the registration desk was pulling on a rope which was strung through the rafters and attached to a large church or school bell, which was now moving back and forth, deafening me — the signal for lunch.

I gave up on the call and joined the line of quilters filing into the dining hall, happy to be anonymous in the crowd. I heard talk about a woman going into the ocean, but it seemed to go nowhere. No one knew who she was. I didn't fill in what I knew. I grabbed my meal and sat at a table where I knew no one, letting the chit chat about sewing machines, grandchildren, and yoga float over my head.

In class, after lunch, the women settled into their seats, cooing and rustling like mourning doves.

Lucy whispered, "I missed you this morning."

I nodded, without explaining where I had been. Lucy didn't look satisfied, but she didn't ask any more questions. I was ready to throw myself into this class, eager to forget the morning's drama. "Where's Harriet?" I asked, noticing for the first time that she wasn't there.

"She didn't come today either," Lucy said. "Not feeling good."

Today, Cinnamon wore jeans and a T-shirt, covered with an oversized man's denim shirt that was dotted with paint.

"We're going to concentrate on the foundation of our piece today," Cinnamon said. She pointed to her three by four feet wall hangings. The goal of the class was to make a similar piece.

"Do you see that the backgrounds are always traditional blocks?"

I strained to see what she was saying. She traced the line of a block on a quilt that featured a fishing pond and small boy. There was so much going on, I hadn't noticed that the backgrounds were made up of pieced blocks. I'd only noticed the subtle changes in colors and textures, not really understanding how those worked in with the large appliqué pieces that made up the story she was telling.

She pointed to another, with a crooked-roofed house. She told us the cherry tree represented her happy childhood as a tomboy, climbing trees and eating fists full of fruit until she got a bellyache. The backgrounds were mostly blues, with a few greens thrown in.

"The best thing you can do is give your quilt layers so that the eye never tires of looking at it. The piecing becomes a treasure, something for the observer to notice only after studying the quilt for a few minutes."

I tried to unfocus my eyes, to see what lay beneath the pictorial elements.

As she pointed to the blocks hidden behind the tree branches, she said, "The block I used here is called 'Hole in the Barn Door,' because the barn on our property has a chunk taken out of it. I've distorted it, changing the angles."

She quickly drew the block on the white-board with the traditional 90-degree angles.

It looked so different. I hadn't known it was the same block.

"Spin it any way you want," she said. "If you use a block that has meaning to you, you will add to the layers of meaning in your quilt."

Lucy said, "I've always liked Storm at Sea. I wonder if I can incorporate that."

"Why not?" I said.

Cinnamon continued, "I have books up here, with pictures and diagrams of traditional blocks. If you're not into that, you could always crazy piece your blocks or use some of the slash-and-piece techniques that don't require matching."

"That's for me," I muttered. Lucy laughed.

"Don't get too hung up on the perfection. I want you to piece these backgrounds quickly and without thinking too much. You should be thinking instead of the story you want to tell."

"If I knew what that was . . ." I muttered.

"I heard that," Cinnamon said. "Don't fret. It's too early to know what you're going to do. In fact, if you have an idea, forget it."

"Oh, so being clueless is a good thing," Lucy said.

"I finally found the right class," I said.

Cinnamon was a good sport and laughed. "Glad to have you."

She whirled around, braid flying, and clapped her hands.

"Let's go. I'm setting the timer for one half-hour. Look at the books. Dig into your fabrics. I will come around and make suggestions. By then, I want you to make your own decisions."

I pulled out the fabrics I'd brought. Most of the quilters had carried in suitcases full of material, with bits and pieces left over from other projects. I felt a little self-conscious with my perfectly cut fat quarters of new fabric lines. My fabric had all been bought at the store in the last week or so. It was obvious to me, and everyone else, how new I was to this. I should have raided my mother's stash. The image of Ursula's crazy quilt robe on the wet, black rocks kept surfacing. I pushed it away. This was my quilt, not hers.

I looked through the pattern books and was drawn to a block called Ocean Waves. It seemed appropriate. It had an awful lot of small triangles, though — too complicated for me. I put the idea out of my head, and moved on.

I had taken the beginning and intermediate quilting classes at the shop with Ina. A death had interrupted my class, but we'd gotten back to the schedule within a couple of weeks. Ina had taught me how to rotary cut safely, how to sew a decent quarter-inch seam allowance, and to measure my borders through the middle of the quilt. I had the basics down. I'd mastered nine patches and gentle curved piecing, and could hand sew an appliqué if someone was holding a gun to my head. I enjoyed it, although not as much as I enjoyed working with Pearl, QP's resident art quilter.

Art quilting meant saying goodbye to the rules. It was okay to use fusing or buttons or beads to cover up mistakes you made. In fact, mistakes were considered design opportunities. I loved that phrase, design opportunities.

But I didn't have Pearl's innate talent. Cinnamon's method of brainstorming and combining old-fashioned piecing with fusible appliqué might work for me.

Suddenly, Cinnamon was at my elbow, her fingers touching my fabric and rifling the edges. She pulled out several, tossing them aside. She changed the position of several others. The pile instantly looked more interesting.

"I'd like to do this block," I said, pointing to a simple nine-patch.

Cinnamon frowned. "Really? That's not very challenging."

"Well, I'm not a great piecer," I said.

"Do you love that block?" she asked.

I had to admit I didn't.

She shook her head. "That won't do. You have to be in love with the block, so that every time you think about sewing, you can't wait to get back to your piece. I want your heart to beat faster every time you work on it."

She licked her thumb and forefinger and paged through the book. "Stop me when you see something you like."

The Ocean Waves block came into view again, and before I could stop myself I laid my finger on it. She looked at me and smiled. "Oh, yes, I can see by your face that you like this one."

"I do," I said, feeling her enthusiasm spill over to me. "But it's a complex block. I'm sure I can't do it," I said.

"The triangles are really tiny, and I'm not a good piecer," I said, feeling my inadequacies weigh me down.

Cinnamon was studying the page. "Let's make it simpler."

I felt a glimmer of hope. Simple I could do. Maybe.

"Picture this," she said, her hands sketching on the handout she'd given us earlier. "One block, blown up to maybe thirty-six inches square."

She quickly drew short lines to represent the triangles. "See, you'd have a large empty space in the middle where you could plant your story quilt. The half-square triangles surrounding it would be big, maybe three, four, even five inches square. That's easy to sew."

I tried to imagine what she was saying. She patted my hand. "You can do this," she said.

With new enthusiasm, I got out the laptop and pulled up the quilting program. I imported one Ocean Waves block and experimented with enlarging it. I could see what Cinnamon meant more clearly on the computer. When the block was made bigger, the middle unpieced block would become the background and the pieced blocks would act as a border. I could handle sewing blocks that were four inches square. I had a much better chance of my points matching if the fabric pieces I started with were not tiny.

I felt a surge of creativity. Cinnamon had really sparked my imagination. Ursula's death seemed far away.

I'd been working steadily for more than an hour when Cinnamon called for our attention.

"It's magic time, girls," Cinnamon trilled, her voice sing-songy. We all looked up expectantly.

"Gather round," the teacher said, setting down a basin of water. "I want you to witness the wonders of cyanotype."

"The what now?" someone asked.

"Behold," Cinnamon said. "In here," she held up a black plastic bag, "is the magic fabric. It will take a snapshot of any object."

"Like sun printing?" someone asked. "Do you use special paints?"

"Nope. It's more akin to photography. Here's one I've already started."

She lifted a piece of cardboard that had been covered in the lime green fabric. On top of that she'd laid shells, several round washers and a fern. "While you people were busy working, I was busy arranging my vignette."

She dipped her fabric square in a basin of water. She was wearing a bracelet of bright yellow plastic bangles that clicked together on her wrist as she swished the fabric around dramatically. The water turned green. She dunked the fabric a final time and wrung it out gently. "Now for the magic part."

"Voila," she said, holding up the dripping piece.

A scene had been printed on the fabric. The words "Positive/Negative" were written across the middle in a funky font. The words were bordered by sea shells and the round washers acted as circular polka dot accents. The fern's feathery appearance softened the piece.

"Wow," the class said as one.

Cinnamon grinned. "Pretty cool. Now, I hate to say this, but that's the end of today's session. Tomorrow you'll get your chance to blueprint."

I was shocked to see it was nearly four o'clock.

"Before you go," Cinnamon said, writing on the white board. "Here's your question for the night."

Cinnamon pointed at the words: "What would you be doing if you weren't here?"

"And one more thing," she passed small sketchbooks around. "One of the best things you can do for your art is work daily," she said.

A groan went up from the group.

"I know you don't think that's possible. It's not always easy getting into our sewing rooms at the end of a long day. But we all can spend a few minutes with our sketchbooks each night."

Lucy nudged me. Cinnamon had passed around her journal. Lucy opened the book and together we looked at her pages. She kept a daily art book, with tiny pictures, and inspirational words. Each page was a work of art that captured a mood, a thought, a feeling with such skill and precision that it took my breath away.

"I can't do this," Lucy said. I agreed.

"I encourage each of you to begin a daily meditation page. If you do a small project each day, you'll start to grow your inner artist," Cinnamon said.

The woman next to me guffawed. "My inner artist? I think she left town with my inner child. And they took my inner millionaire with them."

The whole class laughed. And Cinnamon, to her credit, smiled.

"I know it sounds a little airy fairy, but you all have an artist within. The question is whether or not you do anything to encourage her. Do you paint? Draw? Take a photograph? Even notice when something pretty is around you?"

She frowned as we all looked blankly at her. Clearly, our inner artists were starving for attention.

Cinnamon nodded her head as though she'd made her mind up about something. "That's it. We're taking a field trip tomorrow. Did you all bring digital cameras?"

That had been on the supply list we'd been sent beforehand. Everyone nodded now.

"Bring them and meet me on the boardwalk tomorrow, right after breakfast. We're going to be outside, so dress appropriately."

We walked as a group to the dining hall, laughing as though we'd known each other for years.

The blueprint fabric and the idea of doing a daily sketch were on everyone's mind. We chattered excitedly.

Tony found me waiting in line on the porch. Flashing his badge, he cut in front of the women standing behind. They didn't object. One middle-aged flirt checked out his butt. I frowned at her, and she shrugged. Her friends laughed.

"Busted," one of them said.

Tony was oblivious. He'd have to get used to female attention if he was going to work here.

"Dewey," he said. "Let's talk."

We stepped off the porch.

"What's new?" I asked quietly. "Did Paul Wiggins tell you that he thinks it was his wife?"

"Yes, and the police want to talk to you about that."

"Any word from the Coast Guard?"

He shook his head mournfully. "There's no sign of a body, but the Guard says that's not unusual."

I sighed. It was an unhappy ending to a miserable story. A woman like Ursula, battered and invisible in her adult life — now her body was just as battered and out of sight. Maybe it was just as well I'd never met her.

The determined look on the woman's face in the picture came back to me, though. She'd looked like someone who'd made a decision.

I said, "Her husband really needs to see her body. I doubt he'll ever accept her death otherwise."

"Do you know him? I thought they were from back east," Tony said.

"I met him yesterday," I said, leaving out the real truth of our encounters.

Tony took his hat off and scratched his head. His face was sagging a bit. The search and rescue had taken a toll on him. I wanted to send him home to bed, but I knew better than to try.

"I heard he was a batterer. I don't have a lot of respect for a guy who hits his wife. He was killing her slowly," Tony said.

I nodded. "From everything he says, she was behaving differently the last few months. She wasn't as afraid of him. It sounded like she was standing up to him."

"Maybe it came from the freedom that she'd made up her mind. If she knew she was going to end it, then perhaps she was happier." Tony shrugged. "We'll never know why she threw herself off the cliff."

Suicide? Was it the ultimate in bravery or cowardice? Ending your life if your life was a constant hell? Was that wrong? I would have preferred if she had taken another path, a path that led her away from Paul Wiggins to a life worth living, but I didn't have all the facts. She obviously saw no other way out. Maybe she was in a better place. I couldn't know.

"But why here?" Tony asked.

I looked at him sharply. One look at his face told me he wasn't worrying about his job, he was just puzzling out why Ursula had picked the here and now to end her life.

"This is a special place," I said. "I bet she was happy here once."

I had to think that she'd planned this. That my presence meant nothing. I wouldn't want to think that I'd had anything to do with her choice to jump. I'd stumbled onto an act that was already in the works.

Tony shook himself. "Have you heard from Buster?" Tony asked.

I shook my head slowly. The absence of my cell phone made me ache. I wanted to talk to Buster so badly.

"He'll be down Wednesday," I said. Tomorrow never felt so far away. "I'm sure he'd love to have coffee with you."

My group had moved ahead of me into the dining hall. I started to join them when I remembered I had a question for Tony. "Speaking of coffee, where were you yesterday? You never showed at Juice 'n' Java," I said.

I could barely see Tony's face, but I could tell he was trying to think up something to say.

"Yesterday?" he said weakly. He was stalling for time. That made me more suspicious.

"Yes," I said. "Four o'clock. I risked my driving privileges coming to meet you."

Lost them, too, but that wasn't due to Tony.

"I thought we were supposed to meet at

three," he said.

"No four. After my class." I waited for more of an explanation.

Finally, he said, "Sorry, I got tied up."

"With what? Work?"

I gave him one more chance to explain his whereabouts, but he didn't take it. I remained quiet, just allowing my own silence to tell him I knew he wasn't telling me everything.

"Well, I'm going in to eat," I said, finally.

"Okay, I'm going to my place and crash." His mind was clearly on the investigation.

I joined the others at the table just in time for the tail end of the salad. We got in line for our entrée. Freddy and Quentin were already at the window, plates in hand.

I was chatting with Nan and Sherry. As we got our entrée and moved back into the dining hall, Nan stopped short in front of me.

I looked past her to see what the trouble was.

Freddy had approached Mercedes and was right in her face, his thin body taut with anger. He was a couple of tables over, but we could all hear him clearly. He slammed the surface with his flat hand and leaned forward. I could see the spit gathering in the corner of his mouth.

Mercedes stepped back.

His voice carried. "All I want to do is borrow one of the sewing kits for a few hours. Just to draw the tools for a machine embroidery disc. I wanted to put one out that has the antique tools on it. My customers would snatch that up."

We watched Freddy warily. One of the rangers had her hand on her gun. I wondered if Freddy knew he was being viewed as a risk.

"Nan was okay with it, but you said no, that they were too precious, that you were responsible and couldn't let them out of your sight."

He turned to the ranger. "That was the end of it."

At the front of the room, a man stepped out from behind the half wall that hid the doors from view. My breath caught.

It was Buster.

TEN

His eyes raked the room, checking out the room of quilters. He had his cop face on. He must have been able to hear the angry words on his way in. He'd be unable to relax until he'd assessed the situation. Any new place needed to be vetted for possible threats. He was like a wild animal, alert to any danger at the watering hole.

I left my uneaten dinner on the table. He caught sight of me and waved, his face lighting up. I skipped a step getting to him.

The rangers had quieted Freddy and taken Mercedes and Nan out of the room, heading past the kitchen — probably to hash things out in private. Buster's eyes followed them until they were out of sight.

I flung myself into his arms.

"Everything okay here?" he asked.

"It's just a bunch of quilters," I said, teasing him.

"And we know how harmless they are,"

he said, reminding me we both knew better.

"What are you doing here?" I said. And then I knew. "Tony called you." Tony must have thought I needed Buster after this morning's horror. My brother — always taking care of me. I'd have to thank him later.

"How about a walk?" he said, nodding. "I've been in the car for two hours. Traffic on 101 was brutal."

"Where's your bag? In the car?" I looked around for the duffel he used for overnight trips. "Don't tell me," I said gleefully, "you finally installed a shirt-hanging bar in the truck. I hear seniors get a great discount on those gadgets."

He nudged me. "Funny, girl. I don't think you want to play the age card, do you?"

Buster liked to remind me that he was two years younger when it suited him.

We headed down the meandering paths that led to the beach.

Buster held my hand, his fingers strong and playing with mine. I stuffed his hand in my pocket. The evening air was balmy, feeling warmer than it had this morning. The fog had dissipated. The sun was low in the sky, but it would be light for another hour or so.

"Want to talk about what happened?" he said, his voice soft with concern. The reason

Buster became a cop was because he was empathetic. He spent his life protecting people from getting hurt and stopping those that hurt others. I sometimes wondered if he had enough room in his heart for all the beat-up people in the world.

Buster asked gently, "You saw her go off?"

I took a deep breath. "Well, I turned my head at the last moment, so I didn't see her fall."

"Was she pushed?" he asked.

"No," I said. "No one else was around. It was just me and her."

"Could she have slipped?" he asked.

I shrugged. "I guess."

He shrugged. "Suicides are unpredictable. Some people go deep in the woods so no one will find them. Others are suicides of opportunity. A person will be feeling down and the Golden Gate Bridge is accessible, so over the side they go."

"Whatever it was, it's terribly sad." I felt my voice catch, and brushed against Buster for a comforting second.

"Once her body is found, and the police identify her, they might find the reason. She might have left a note for her family somewhere."

I nestled my head under his chin and pressed my body against his. I let his breathing steady me and forced all the images of Ursula out of my mind. There was no help for her now. I felt myself return to normal. I pulled back and looked in Buster's eyes.

"How about coming back to my room?"

I could see he was frowning, his brows knitted. My heart sank. That was his game face, when he had bad news for me. "What?" I said. "Spit it out."

He squeezed my hand. "I can't stay the night. I've got to be in court in the morning."

I walked a few steps away, rocked by the news. "Oh, Buster, come on." I was so disappointed I couldn't say anymore without crying. My hopes had gotten so high, then dashed. I hadn't realized until that moment how much I'd wanted to wake up next to him in the morning.

He shrugged, his shoulders wide in his sweatshirt. The man was smart enough to wear blue a lot. It was hard to stay mad at him when his eyes looked so good, true and clear.

"Duty calls," he said.

I glanced at my watch. It was seven o'clock. "Let's keep going." I didn't want to waste time being mad at him, but I needed to work off some of this resentment.

"Let's go see the golf course," he said. "I

scored a two o'clock tee time at Del Monte. For Saturday, after your conference."

My spirits lifted.

"And I got us reservations at the Cypress Inn for Friday night and Saturday," he continued. He was obviously proud of himself.

The Cypress Inn was impossible to get into. I'd been wanting to go there for years. There was a hot tub for two that looked out over the Pacific.

I decided to forgive him.

"You totally rock," I said, jumping on his back for a piggy-back ride down the street. Buster jogged along, hugging the side of the road and dumping me at the entrance to the walking path, a couple hundred yards away, the opposite direction that I'd gone that morning.

We held hands and walked. His hands were large and I liked the way my palm nestled into his. I stroked it with my finger. There was no place I'd rather be than with Buster. I loved that he'd gotten us into a fancy hotel this weekend, but I'd have stayed in a yurt at Los Pinos State Park with him if he'd asked.

The path led us through high bushes and onto a wooden bridge over a creek. Foliage filled the creek bed. Water trickled through.

We couldn't see the ocean from here, but its rhythms underscored our quiet. The deep call of sea lions sounded like a fog horn warning against the treacherous rocks.

"There's no place I'd rather be right now," Buster whispered in my ear, echoing my own thoughts. We'd stopped at the bridge and he stood behind me, his hands gripping the redwood railing on either side of me. A frog croaked deeply and we heard a splash as it returned to the water.

I looked up, and he kissed my outstretched neck. Sparks shot down my body, my toes lifted involuntarily off the ground. Buster leaned against me, his whole body shielding me. I loved the hardness of his body against mine, and I turned in his arms as his lips continued their journey, reaching the vulnerable dip in my collarbone.

Buster pushed his knee into my thighs, as though he could hold me up if I needed him to.

And I might need him to.

After a few minutes of this, I pushed him away. Buster's hand was under my shirt, and he'd managed to get the top of my pants undone. I was breathing hard.

"Hold on, it's a long way back to my room," I said. "If you keep this up, I won't be able to walk."

"It's completely private here," he said. "No one can see us."

The bullfrog protested. I laughed. "He can," I said. "Let's just walk some more." I straightened my clothes, and snapped my pants.

Buster leaned off me and, taking my hand, led me over the bridge. He walked ahead of me several steps. I saw him adjust his pants with his free hand. Poor guy. I smiled.

A few yards down, a golf hole appeared on our left, bright green. Buster stopped to study it, as though he could determine the best way to play an imaginary lie. I pulled him ahead.

I wanted to see the water. Suddenly we were over a dune, and the ocean was in view. The beach was full of people. A dreadlocked girl was sitting on a piece of driftwood playing guitar. We heard snatches of "Sweet Baby James" before the wind shifted.

The path curled around the golf course, giving us glimpses of perfectly groomed greens and raked sand traps. Beyond, highrise hotels lined the distance. Asilomar was right next to million-dollar properties where the greens fees were over four hundred dollars and hotel rooms cost upward of a thousand dollars a night. I was paying a little over a hundred and thirty. With meals

135

included.

Thank you, State of California.

We watched the sunset from a slight rise over the beach. The sky turned orange, then red, and back to orange. Buster pretended to hiss when the sun dropped below the horizon.

Once the sun had gone down, the beach grew empty as people packed up their picnics and headed for home.

We walked back the way we came. It was extremely quiet. Darkness had fallen quickly. We stopped at the bridge again.

Buster pointed out the first star that came out. "Make a wish," he said.

Stay with me tonight, I thought. I didn't want to complain, but the idea of going back to my room alone was hard.

"You should start for home," I said instead. "I don't want you exhausted for tomorrow."

"It won't take long to get back to San Jose at this hour," Buster said. "I'll be fine."

He nuzzled my ear, and let his lips dip lower. "Or I could stay with you until dawn and go straight to work from here."

"In those clothes?" I said, faux-horrified. "The same clothes you wore today. As if, you'd ever . . ."

"I could wash out my unmentionables in

136

your sink," Buster said. As distracted as he was by the slightly freckled skin between my breasts, the man could still think laundry.

I laughed. His head came up, nearly hitting my chin. I ducked away.

"Are you deliberately trying to wreck the mood?" he asked, rubbing the side of his face with his big hand. He looked tired. I was going to send him home.

"The mood?"

He pouted. "I drove all the way here to see you."

I turned into his embrace and kissed him back. I opened my mouth to his, our tongues playing. His kisses grew more urgent. He slipped my shirt off my shoulder, baring it. His lips smoothed the goosebumps away and I shivered. His arms tightened. I felt him grow beneath the zipper of his pants. The bulge excited me, and I felt myself moisten.

I undid the buckle of my belt and Buster took over, finding the snap and zipper with one skilled hand. He pushed my shirt away from my waistband, bending over to kiss the soft skin of my belly. I felt myself suck in, as his lips hit my cold skin. The hot and cold sensations were too much to bear. His mouth was moving closer to my tenderest spot. I gasped as he licked my belly button.

His hands shimmied my pants down, and I grabbed at his. He leaned me hard against the wood railing. A splintery piece of wood stabbed my lower back, the skin vulnerable. Buster misunderstood my gasp and redoubled his efforts, moving his fingers inside my pants. His tender administrations were too hard to resist. I didn't feel the rough wood anymore.

The frog protested, but I smelled wild blackberry and the musk on Buster's neck, and I let him in.

ELEVEN

It was after ten when Buster and I got back to Asilomar. A raccoon scooted out of a barbecue pit as we passed. Chicken bones and garbage were strewn around the bricks.

"Dirty bastard," Buster said. I looked at him in surprise. He was more tired than he was letting on.

He frowned. "They're scavengers," he said. I got the idea he wasn't telling me something. Buster had been on plenty of body identifications. I suddenly wondered what else raccoons might have gnawed on.

The parking spot Buster had found was in the underground garage all the way across the campus from my room. I walked with him, already missing him.

Once there, Buster kissed my cheek, and opened his truck door and got in. I climbed up on the step and kissed him back, letting my hand trail over his cheek.

"I wish you didn't have to go," I said.

"I'll drive you back to your room," he said.

I shook my head. "No thanks, I could use the walk."

I waved as he took off. I started in the direction of my room.

After a few minutes, I wasn't sure I'd made the right choice. It was dark now, and street lights were far apart. The paths of Asilomar were meandering. Right now I wished for a straight line back to my dorm — a well-lit straight line.

The asphalt path was cracked and uneven. I could hear the unstoppable ocean and imagined wave after wave coming to shore. The moon was in and out of the clouds, leaking a teasing brightness that was impossible to follow. I picked my way carefully. I heard a rustling in the small clearing and remembered the mountain lion. My feet stopped of their own volition.

The rangers warned us about going out at night. And here I was. Alone.

I felt silly and scared and missed Buster already. Could the cat smell me? Ina had a standard warning for beginning quilters that their sewing machines could smell their fear, so they had to act like they knew what they were doing, even when they didn't know their feed dogs from their take-up hook.

But how was I supposed to behave in the face of a mad mountain lion? Act large, wave arms about? Yell and scream. Tony had told me about singing in the meadows of Yosemite to keep the grizzlies away. He said they hated anything by Barry Manilow.

I couldn't think of any Barry Manilow songs. I couldn't think of anything, really.

A long shadow crossed my path. I nearly screamed, but my voice wouldn't come out. The shadow was low to the ground, and definitely had four legs.

My heart stopped for a moment, as a deer crossed my path, ten feet away. I took in a deep breath and tried to restore my heart to its normal rhythm.

The path ahead of me suddenly brightened. I could see light spilling from the open door of Merrill Hall. As I got closer, I could see groups of quilters lingering outside. Most were in heavy sweatshirts and sweatpants against the night chilled air.

"What's going on?" I approached the first group.

"We're not being told anything," Sherry said. "Mini-Mer said to get over here pronto."

"Mini-Mer?" I asked.

"Mercedes' assistant. She's a clone of her boss. She came around, banging on doors and telling us to meet in Merrill Hall. But they won't let us in."

"I, for one, don't appreciate missing my beauty sleep," Harriet said. She was wearing pajamas with tiny moons and stars and alarm clocks on them. Her feet were in pink sheepskin slippers. I was surprised to see her, but glad she hadn't gone home.

Others must have been sewing — their clothes were sprinkled with threads, and some of them carried small scissors.

"You'd have to sleep for a hundred years to get to the beauty part," Red said, stepping into the light. Harriet threw a soft punch in her direction which Red dodged and then gathered her into a reconciliatory hug. "You know you're gorgeous," she said.

"Another mandatory meeting?" I asked. I hadn't considered that Mercedes might have bed checks. Good thing Buster hadn't actually made it to my room. My face flamed, and I was glad it was too dark for everyone to see.

The main doors to the hall opened and we were directed inside. The space was similar to the chapel, with over arching beams of timber and tall skinny windows, but it was much bigger. The crowd didn't fill a fourth of the floor space.

There was no sign of Mini-Mer, just Mercedes and the sewing machine tool expert, Nan. Both looked gloomy. Nan had put distance between herself and Mercedes, standing on the opposite side of the stage.

Freddy and Quentin found me as we filed into the room. Quentin was dressed in pajamas with matching corduroy slippers and a monogrammed robe. His several hairs were laid carefully over his bald pate. He was only missing a pipe, which I was sure he would have had if Mercedes allowed smoking on the premises.

I waggled an eyebrow in Quentin's direction at Freddy. He glanced at his outfit and smiled slightly, but he was clearly not in the mood to dish on his friend. My need for a joke to break the ice was not forthcoming. I rubbed my upper arms.

I'd missed the dinner chat. Had there been any mention of Ursula being swept out to sea? Maybe that's what this was about.

"Please find a seat," Mercedes said. "Quickly and quietly."

A woman swathed in a scarf, topped by a wide-brimmed hat, stepped onto the stage and whispered in Mercedes' ear. The woman had her hands tucked into the sleeves of her oversized sweater, looking like

Mother Superior. We were clearly the novitiates.

Mercedes' voice rang out in the spacious hall: "There is a thief among us."

Twelve

Mercedes' dramatic statement hung in the air. All talking ceased abruptly as though the oxygen had been sucked out of the room.

She didn't need the microphone. Her voice projected across the large room easily. Probably an architectural trick — the acoustics were really good in here. "I'm sorry to report two of the precious antique sewing kits have been stolen."

A gasp went up from the crowd. People stood, some trying to see Nan's distress more closely. Freddy emitted a low whistle.

Mercedes looked grave. "If any one of you has something to tell us, please do so now. We will wait. I would like to give the thief a chance to return the boxes."

Mercedes said nothing further. Her assistant faded into the darkness of the stage. Nan wrung her hands, her expression pleading.

"Is she planning on keeping us here until someone confesses?" I whispered to Freddy. I resented the idea.

"I wouldn't be surprised if she starts administering lie detector tests."

"I guess we should be grateful we're not being waterboarded," Quentin said.

"God, don't give her any ideas," Freddy hissed.

For a few moments there was silence, interrupted only by the rustling of bodies shifting uncomfortably. Mercedes looked out at the crowd as though expecting some kind of miraculous revelation. I didn't see anyone who looked like they were ready to confess.

I raised my hand. I'd been involved in real police interrogations. I would move this process along. Mercedes acknowledged me.

"When were the kits last seen?" I asked. "And where?"

"Go, Sherlock, go," Freddy said.

"I prefer Nancy Drew," I said, under my breath. "Or Pippi Longstocking."

"Even I know she wasn't a detective," Freddy whispered. I hushed him.

Mercedes was willing to play along. "In the chapel, which has been locked up tight since Monday night."

Nan looked heartbroken. She had taken a

seat at the edge of the stage, swinging her legs nervously. She swiped at her eyes from time to time. She was trying to hold it together.

"Which kits are missing?" I asked.

"The Rose Box," Mercedes paused for effect, "and the German Cross."

A wave of chatter went through the room, everyone reacting with horror.

Eyes turned to Harriet, who blushed deeply. She pushed up roughly from her seat and stood up. She started to speak, but the whispers grew so loud, she couldn't be heard. Harriet, struggling to look dignified in her pink pj's, walked to the front of the room.

She took the microphone and turned it on.

"I did not steal that abominable piece of work. I would not sully my hands by touching it. I'd like to say I'm sorry, but I'm not. I hope that the thief has dashed that horror into a million little pieces on the rocks."

The quilters looked at her in stunned silence. Harriet held my gaze until she finally looked at Mercedes with disgust. "I hope it has washed out to sea."

Nan looked stricken, the idea of her precious collectible being swept out to sea too much to bear. She wrapped her arms tightly around her body.

Harriet left the microphone on the podium and walked out the side door. Sherry and Red got up and followed her. Mercedes watched them leave.

Her eyes raked the crowd.

"If you're trying to punish me, I assure you that I will in no way accept responsibility for the stolen kit."

Nan looked at her, a strangled look on her face. Her voice, soft at first, grew in volume and anger. "This is *your* responsibility. You assured me my things would be safe here. You guaranteed me that my . . . ," her voice broke, and her words were unintelligible until she breathed out the last word in a huge sigh, "Safe."

Safety. What we all wanted.

Mercedes silenced Nan with a look. "I insist that you all remain here until the kit is returned."

I settled back after Harriet's friends left. The rest of the quilters were not eager to confront Mercedes.

What would this do to her reputation? Part of the draw of Sewing-by-the-Sea was the international teachers she'd attracted. Many of them brought their most valuable quilts, valued in the tens of thousands of dollars. They were on display for all to see, hanging in the classrooms the entire week. I'd recognized Cinnamon's pieces as prize winners. What if one of those got stolen?

I looked around. I didn't see Cinnamon, my teacher, or any other teachers except Freddy. He was practically humming with excitement. His birdlike head kept twisting, trying to see all parts of the room. I'd meant to ask him what the hubbub was at the dining hall earlier. He'd wanted to borrow the boxes. Which ones?

Quentin, next to him, was very still. He sat with his head in his hands, elbows on his knees.

After twenty minutes of no activity, I was getting angry about being accused. I had nothing to do with this and I wanted to crawl into my bed. My body ached with fatigue.

Being kept until nearly midnight for this bogus inquiry began to wear on the rest of the crowd, too.

A woman in the middle, dressed in a pink seersucker robe and matching curlers, stood. "I'm going to bed," she announced. Several women stood in her row and headed for the door.

"The doors are locked," Mercedes warned.

The processional stopped.

Enough. I jumped up. "Unlock them," I said. "You can't keep us in here. There are laws against unlawful imprisonment."

Mercedes stared at me with an imperious glare. She didn't move for a minute. I returned her look. Finally, she moved to the door and unlocked it with a key she produced from a pocket. She stood outside the door, scrutinizing each person as they left.

Mercedes stopped me, as I passed her, giving me a proprietary jab on the arm. "I'm watching you," she said.

"What's that supposed to mean?" I asked.

"I know what you've done. You've stolen the sewing box just to stir the pot. You're a troublemaker of the highest order. I will not take this quietly."

People began to stop, listening to Mercedes' accusation. My face reddened. I could think of no snappy comeback. Freddy pushed me from behind, past Mercedes and her accusations.

THIRTEEN

The next morning at breakfast, the conversation was all about the missing sewing boxes. I felt queasy from the upset the night before, and I was glad Harriet was not at breakfast.

I let the talk wash over me, without really listening, wondering if anyone had heard anything about Ursula. I decided to ask around.

Over a glass of chocolate milk, I asked Sherry, "Did you know Ursula Wiggins? She used to come here to the seminar."

Sherry searched her memory, but came up empty. She shook her head. "Maybe if I saw her," she offered. "Why, do you think she stole the sewing kits?"

It was my turn to shake my head. "No." I didn't want to ruin her breakfast by telling her about the suicide. We were all unsettled by the thefts and Mercedes' heavy-handedness.

"What about the Ghost?" Red asked as she joined us. "Maybe the Ghost was the thief."

"I doubt it. I think the Ghost is a woman who just enjoys her downtime," Sherry said.

"No torrid romance?" Red wondered.

Sherry laughed. "You know as well as I do, when you get to our age, an empty bed can be more alluring than a stiffy."

I gave up on turning the conversation to Ursula. The atmosphere was one of determined levity. No one wanted to be reminded of the seriousness of the theft.

I heard a roar of laughter come from a table across the room. Freddy was standing, shaking his hips and moving his hands in a way that suggested a hula. The women, and Quentin, were clapping in unison as Freddy strutted. He segued into a Mick Jagger chicken walk. Someone whistled appreciatively.

I had time before class so I decided to walk out to the ocean where I'd first seen the VW bus parked. I walked to the water's edge and stood on a rock.

I spread my arms out, Titanic-style, like Ursula had, and felt the wind waffle through the sleeves of my sweatshirt. It was cold, and wet, feeling like a dog's kiss. I shivered and my arms came back in to cradle me.

"Why here?" I asked. I looked up and down the coast. Why at Asilomar?

She could have killed herself with carbon monoxide in her garage, in the house she shared with her abusive husband. She could have taken pills and died in her bed. She could have shot herself in the head. Instead she flew halfway across the country and jumped into the ocean. Why?

The answer had to be at Sewing-by-the-Sea. Paul had insinuated as much. It was the only thing that made sense.

I walked back toward Asilomar along the road. Again, the berm was covered with cars. Just like yesterday morning.

Only one group of people was out as early as I'd been yesterday. Surfers. Maybe one of them had seen or talked to Ursula.

They sat on the side of the road, alone, or in groups of two or three, talking quietly, waiting for the surf to grow. Right now the waves looked gentle. Several surfers could be seen paddling out.

"Hey guys," I said.

"Good morning, missy," a pony-tailed veteran said, flashing a smile that was missing a tooth. His now-dry wetsuit hung below his flabby belly. On his feet were neoprene slippers. He looked like a fish out of water.

Several other surfers looked my way. One brought a cereal bowl up to his mouth and noisily slurped. Another held his cigarette behind his back. I could smell pot. I sniffed the air. I had to shake off a sensory memory of a college soiree.

"Were you out here yesterday?" I asked.

"We're out here every day," the grizzly man said. "We're hard-core."

Just like the quilters.

"I figured," I said, trying to make it sound like a compliment. "I saw a woman down there yesterday." I pointed in the direction of the cliffs, a quarter mile up the beach. The coastline curved right here, and the cliff where she went off was not visible.

"Did any of you see her? Talk to her?" It was a long shot, but she had to come from somewhere. Maybe she'd walked this way.

"She had long, red curly hair, kind of wild," I said, appealing to their esthetic. "And she was wearing a long cape, crazy quilt style."

I was drawing nothing but blank looks.

"Crazy?" one of them said, but it was only a comment on the world at large.

The surfers looked at each other blankly, and returned to looking over my shoulder at the shore line. It was obvious these guys saw nothing that didn't relate to the waves, the conditions, the clouds.

I remembered the van that had gone past me on my way back to Asilomar. I wasn't sure it had anything to do with Ursula, but the timing was right. These were guys. I should have started with the mechanical, not people.

I said, "How about the van? Did you see a gray VW bus go by?"

Eyes perked up. A young guy brushed his long hair out of his eye. It was covering half his face. I felt old standing next to him, resisting the urge to hook his locks behind his ears so I could see his face. God, it was awful being thirty.

"A Vanagon?" he asked.

I shrugged. "I don't know."

He said to his buddies, "I saw a bitchin' Synchro pull up when I was leaving yesterday."

"I thought that was Cotati's," the old guy said.

"Nah, his got repossessed. Anyway, this one was silver."

"That's it," I said. I mentally kicked myself; I should have known to start with the car. I've got enough men in my family to know that cars are a common language. Most of my deeper conversations with my

Dad started with queries about the oil in my car.

"Did you see where it went?" I needed an accurate description of the car to take to the police.

No one answered.

"Where's this Cotati guy?" I asked, looking around at the pick-ups and vans parking along the road. A group was grilling breakfast sausages on the side of the road. The smell was tantalizing and my stomach growled.

"Don't see him." Hairy guy shrugged. "Maybe later," he said. "He's always here if the surf is good."

I looked out at the placid sea. "Is the surf going to be good?"

Sleepy-eyes said, "Depends if the gods are smiling on us, man."

Surf philosophy was more than I could handle so early in the day. The sausage smell was joined by grilled bananas. I felt my mouth water, even though I'd just eaten.

"Have you seen a well-dressed, gray-haired guy walking along here?" I asked.

"You mean that dude whose woman went in the drink?" The question came from a new guy whose tattoos covered both arms completely.

I was surprised. "Yes, that's him. Did you

talk to him?"

From the smell of pot that lingered in the air like a not-so-fresh air freshener, I doubted these guys would have any sense of time or be good informational sources, but I needed to find Paul.

"Yesterday. Man, was he bummed out. The ocean, man, it's a killer."

I waited for something more succinct, but the surfer was lost in his thoughts, staring out at the waves, and mindlessly banging his fingers against his thighs. I wondered what was so frightening in his life that he dulled his senses with pot and surfed in the very essence of what terrified him.

"Did you see him today?" I asked.

Another surfer looked up from waxing his board and said, "He was walking past the golf course when I drove in this morning."

We were surrounded by golf courses. To the north was Pacific Grove Muni. To the south were the exclusive Pebble Beach courses, where Buster and I had walked last night. He pointed south.

Ursula had gone in north of where we were. I could see a figure standing on the sand, staring out to sea. Was that Paul?

"Thanks," I said, heading to the shoreline. I'd walk on the packed sand near the water and make faster progress.

He didn't see me at first. His eyes were on the water, watching each wave as it hit the short jetty.

"Any word?" I said. No matter what else he was, right now, Paul was a man grieving his wife.

He blinked, looking at me with unseeing eyes.

"How goes the investigation?" I asked.

"It's over," Paul said.

"Over?" I asked. "What do you mean?"

"They're finished. There's no sign of her body."

The terrain looked so different from the way it had in the early morning fog when I'd seen her go over. Today the water was sparkling blue, with green translucent stripes, like a wonderful batik. The white caps had calmed down and the waves gently moved in.

The ocean looked serene, but it was teeming with life. The same was true for Paul. His exterior was calm, but his guts had to be churning.

The sky was a bright blue, and several clouds scudded across but without breaking up the bright day. The black rocks, the white sands, the wildflowers, the craggy coastline were all the makings of a dream. But for Paul, it was a nightmare.

"What was she doing here? Mercedes told me Ursula hadn't attended the conference the last couple of years."

"She did. she came every year. I wrote the check, and booked her ticket. For the past ten years. The second week in May. I put her on the plane myself."

I thought about what he was saying. "At the airport, did you drop her at the gate? Or just at the curb?"

I saw his face change as he recognized that he didn't know where she flew to. She could have turned in her ticket for a new destination, paying cash for any penalties.

He must have hated it when the airport rules changed. I was sure before that he'd walked her to her plane and stayed until take-off.

He thought for a moment, his hand stroking the stubble he'd been growing. He'd let himself go these last two days and didn't resemble the dapper man I'd met on Monday. His hair was dirty, plastered to the back of his head, and his fingernails were bleeding at the cuticles.

I almost felt sorry for him. He was a batterer, yes, but wife beaters weren't created in a vacuum. Who knew what kind of life he'd had? What things in his past had led him to this path?

I couldn't forgive him for making his wife's life hell, but he was in his own kind of torment. He would never be able to right things with Ursula now. He could only wait for her body to be found.

"How do you even know she came here? She could have gone anywhere."

He turned to me with a triumphant look. "Each year, she brings me an edition of the local paper."

That was proof of sorts. *The Pacific Grove Bulletin* was not readily available. I had never seen it outside of a couple of shops right in town. She must have been here. At least in Pacific Grove.

His eyes had been drawn back to the endless sea. His mouth was drawn into a frown and his eyes were vacant. He was watching the horizon as though Ursula would pop up, like a sea otter.

He said he didn't believe she'd gone in voluntarily, but he couldn't keep his eyes off the water.

"Why was Ursula in California, Paul?"

"I told you," his voice was muffled as he curled into himself. "She was taking the Sewing-by-the-Sea seminar. I wrote the check myself. It was cashed months ago."

That was interesting. Paul had given fifteen hundred dollars to Mercedes for a phantom registration. In the past, the Ghost had paid for the class, shown up on the first morning, and then wasn't seen again until the last night. Everyone assumed she had a boyfriend. But what if she didn't have a boyfriend at all? What if she was just trying to get away from an abusive husband once a year?

A woman like Ursula would have no money of her own. Paul probably controlled all the money coming in and going out. Where would a woman like that get money? From Mercedes.

Paul wasn't moving, just kept staring at one spot as though waiting for something to surface.

My mother used to write a check at the grocery store for ten or twenty dollars over the amount of her purchases. She called the change she got back her "mad" money. Dad thought it was money she'd spent on groceries, and she had a little cash she could call her own. It never got spent on anything more than socks for us kids or an occasional lunch out with a girlfriend or a gift for my dad, but it was important to her to have some money she didn't have to account for. And my father was not a tyrant.

I could only imagine what lengths a woman in Ursula's position might go to get some mad money.

It was easy to fall in love with a place like Asilomar. The ocean breezes, sculpted cypress trees, the cute sea otters, the healing balm of the repetition of the waves. Why wouldn't a woman come back year after year?

How hard it must have been to go home each time. Knowing what she was going back to. Did he promise to be good? Did he swear never to touch her in anger again? Was she fooled time and time again by his inability to stop?

There had to have come a time when she said enough was enough. Paul had said he'd been treating her well in the last few years. What if he'd suffered a relapse last year, and she decided to make the break once and for all.

It could have taken her a year to get the resources she needed to escape.

I needed to get my hands on Mercedes' registrations.

Paul spoke, startling me. "My wife has been killed," he said. "Murdered."

I said, "I saw her. She was alone. She wasn't pushed."

"There was a man after her, making her life miserable."

I didn't believe him. Only one man had

tortured Ursula. He was standing right next to me.

I pointed down the beach.

"If you loved your wife so much, why are you out here, instead of down there where she went in?"

Paul turned to me. His eyes were hooded and his face expressionless. "The police said it might take days, but bodies usually get hung up on that sand bar. And surface right here."

FOURTEEN

"Ready to go take some legendary pictures?" Cinnamon asked. She looked like Jimmy Olsen, with huge cameras and lenses hanging from leather straps around her neck. The rest of us, gathered in front of the classroom, were carrying palm-sized digitals.

"Let's go off to the dunes," Cinnamon said. "I want you to start seeing what's right in front of you."

We headed through the trees, on a bark path I hadn't noticed before. It led past the sleeping rooms and around the back of the Mott Ranger training station. We crossed Sinex Road and went through the parking lots surrounding other classrooms. Through the windows, I could see quilts hanging on walls. One group was outside dyeing fabric, using a makeshift clothesline to hang colorful newly created pieces.

We talked as we walked. Harriet told me

about her ideas for her legendary quilt, a family tree honoring the women on her mother's side. She was subdued, but I was glad she'd come to class. Lucy told me she didn't want to hide away.

A raven squawked, and I could smell the salt air. The dunes were just ahead. I felt a lifting in my heart. What a cool thing to be doing on a normal week day. Spending hours outdoors instead of hunched over my computer. I let the images fade of Paul Wiggins staring out to sea and Nan wringing her hands over her missing kit.

Here the seagulls greeted us, and the pelicans performed their Rockettes routine, flying in an impossibly straight line, dipping as one. Cinnamon had the right idea. I never stopped to smell the roses, never mind trying to imitate them in fabric. I was daunted by the task, but energized at the prospect that I might create something unique and meaningful.

After ten minutes of pointing out the minute flowers in the sand dunes, showing us the tiny bugs and the deer tracks, Cinnamon broke us apart.

"I'll give you one hour, people. Use your time to take pictures that appeal to you. I don't want you shooting what I've shown you or looking over your neighbor's shoulders to see what they're doing."

We laughed as she leered at the closest student as she demonstrated.

Her smile disappeared.

"I'm serious. This is the chance to make something unique. Just for you. We share our homes, our workspaces, with spouses and friends and children. Now is the time to find your vision. I don't care what it is, as long as it's uniquely yours."

The idea of making a quilt about something important in my life had never occurred to me before. Most of the quilts I'd seen were made from quilt blocks, set together in interesting patterns with cool fabrics. A few landscape quilts came into the store. One I remembered was a replica of the Vatican. I'd seen memory quilts, too made with specially treated fabric that transferred pictures onto cotton or silk. Last year a customer had showed us one she made for her parents, celebrating sixty years of marriage. The pictures had run the gamut from baby pictures and vacation shots to their original wedding day photo.

But this was different. Cinnamon's idea was to recreate a feeling, a thought.

In college, trying to decide my major, I'd taken a Chart Your Life seminar. For a weekend, we cut up magazines. The goal was to find pictures that appealed to us and use them to collage our heart's desires. The idea was that beneath the conscious minds were wants and needs that we were barely aware of. Mine had been a jumble of disconnected images and trite sayings used as ad copy. I'd learned nothing about my ambitions or myself.

Despite the splendor of the outdoors, I knew what I wanted to photograph. The stone and wood that made up the original historical buildings. The thirteen remaining buildings that Julia Morgan had built nearly a hundred years ago. She'd managed to merge man-made structures into the natural beauty. I wanted to try to capture that.

I started in the chapel, concentrating on the windows that framed the dunes beyond. I shot the frieze and the graceful choir loft. I moved on to the Lodge. In the living room, I took pictures of the elegant staircase.

Next up was the Administration building. The historical placard told me this had once been the Phoebe Hearst Social Hall. Here was where the young women arrived by train to spend their summers at Asilomar. I could only imagine what it meant to have this kind of recreation available to a young woman in the 1920s. I sensed it was a freedom that I, who'd never been repressed, could not begin to appreciate.

I moved around the massive river rock fireplace, zooming in on the vertical pieces Julia Morgan had added for stability. They added beauty as well.

Someone was playing the piano. I didn't know the tune being played, but it was slow and sad. I glanced over at the player, recognizing her with a jolt. It was Nan.

I walked over to her. "Hi, Nan," I said.

She looked my way, her eyes sad. "Hi, Dewey."

"I'm sorry about the boxes going missing. Please know I had nothing to do with that."

She nodded glumly, her fingers caressing the piano keys. I was interrupting her mourning. Her chin dimpled as though she might cry.

"I know it wasn't you," she said.

I didn't know what else to say, but I felt awkward just leaving her.

She finished her song, arms and shoulders getting into the act.

She shut the piano lid with an abrupt crash. "It's not right. That box was made in Pennsylvania more than a hundred years ago. It has nothing to do with politics."

"Is that why you think the German Cross was stolen?" I asked.

"Why else?" she said.

"But what about the other box? Is the Rose Box valuable?"

She shook her head. "Not really. Remember? One of the tools was missing."

I nodded. I did remember. It had a tray that nested in the box. Each piece had its own slot, the exact shape of the tool. The design was the height of efficiency. There could be no misplaced tools. It reminded me of my dad's pegboard in the garage. He'd outlined the shape of each tool that hung there. He'd done that when we kids were little, to ensure that the tool got returned to its proper place. He could see at a glance what was missing, then send us kids out to look for it. It was usually under Kevin's bed, or on his desk, until Dad built him his own tool bench.

Tony had never borrowed Dad's tools, preferring the camp stove and Coleman lantern.

"But how does that affect the value?" I asked.

"If the kit is incomplete, the value goes way down. Some of the boxes I displayed had their tools replaced long ago. But the Rose Box is almost intact, except for that one missing bird."

Nan's fingers caressed the piano hinge.

"The Rose Box is the most beautiful piece I own. The workmanship is amazing and it is one of a kind, but without the missing sewing bird, it's practically worthless. I believe whoever took it was trying to hide the fact that she was really after the German Cross box."

Harriet, in other words.

"Has stuff gone missing in other years? I've heard about quilts being stolen."

"From Sewing-by-the-Sea?" Nan grew thoughtful. "Let me think. I think there was a Featherweight sewing machine that someone lost."

"There are a lot of expensive quilts hanging on the walls of rooms that are open all day."

"But they're locked up every night. And most of the time, those rooms are full of students."

"I know. I'm thinking of the woman, the Ghost, who comes every year but doesn't attend class. Maybe she helps herself to people's things. That's why she stays anonymous."

"That's horrible," Nan said. Her voice quavered, and she put a hand up to cover her mouth. I touched her arm, and she forced a smile.

"I'm sure the police will find the thief,"

she said bravely.

I admired her naiveté. She thought the police would be working hard to discover who'd stolen her prized possessions. I wasn't going to burst her bubble.

Nan paged through the songbook, looking for a new piece to play. I felt like an intruder, so I said my goodbyes and continued on my way.

Right at eleven, my class gathered on the wide porch of the Administration building. I could hear the piano. Nan had started another mournful tune.

Cinnamon was holding a bundle wrapped in black plastic. "Everyone got their shots?" she shouted, to be heard over the ocean and Nan.

We roared back our enthusiastic replies.

"Good. Now put your cameras away."

We groaned. We'd been pumped.

"We're going to capture an image another way," Cinnamon said.

She handed out the small packages. "Don't open it yet," she warned.

When she was finished, she held up hers. "Remember the blueprint I showed you yesterday? Now it's your turn. In this package is a piece of the specially treated fabric."

I felt a frisson of anticipation sweep the group. I was excited, too. This class was challenging me in ways I hadn't imagined. I was full of the genius of Julia Morgan and feeling my own creative urges awaken.

"You looked at the macro world and the micro world, now I want you to focus on one object," Cinnamon said. "An interesting shape, a profile. Whatever. Just think beyond the gingko leaf or the fern or the sand dollar."

One woman said, "Darn!"

"You were headed straight for the tide pool, am I right?" Cinnamon said. The woman nodded ruefully.

"Think different."

The woman scowled as though she was thinking hard, cracking up the rest of us.

A picture was coming into my mind, one of the artifacts I'd seen in one of these buildings. A skeleton key, beautifully shaped.

I tried to remember where I'd seen it, while listening to the directions from Cinnamon.

"I've given you a piece of the fabric taped to cardboard. Write your name on the scotch tape I've put on your piece. Don't expose it to the light until you've got your image in place. Take your object, lay it on the specially treated fabric and expose it for at least ten minutes. You won't be able to see much. You've got to have faith."

I gathered my bundle to my chest.

Cinnamon clapped her hands. "We'll rinse them later. You've got forty-five minutes until lunch. I can't wait to see what you come up with. Don't disappoint me."

The plaque on the side of the building read "Pirates' Den." It explained that the men who had been brought to the all-girl YWCA camp to teach the women how to drive had been quartered here.

My car keys were trapped in there. There was something fitting about that. But now I was in search of a different key. I thought I knew where I'd seen the key. In Mercedes' office.

The building sat on a slope. On the first floor were the living room and several sleeping rooms and the public bathrooms. Down a level were several more sleeping rooms. One room sat by itself, on the lower level, isolated from the other dorm rooms by the hill.

Neither Mercedes or her assistant was in sight now.

What I wanted was in the living room. On the wall by the bathroom was a closet door, painted the same beige color as the walls. Slotted in the keyhole was an old-fashioned brass key, now dark with age and human handling. Right where I remembered it. I congratulated myself.

I pulled the key out and held it up. It was at least four inches long, rounded at the filigreed bottom. The notches were cut with precision, forming interesting nooks and crannies. It was perfect for this project.

I opened the blueprint fabric, trying to remember what Cinnamon had said about the sun exposure. I pulled out the cardboard, dropping the black plastic bag that it'd been in. I laid the key on the green fabric, and opened the curtain to let in the light.

I bent down to pick up the bag that had drifted to the ground.

A Polaroid print lay on the floor under the desk where Mercedes had been sitting at the other day. I picked it up, bringing it close to the window so I could see it.

It was a picture of the Rose Box, taken in this room. I could see the curtains in the background. The box had been sitting on the table in front of the window and lay on top of a copy of *The Pacific Grove Bulletin,* positioned so that the date was showing. The newspaper was today's edition.

It looked like a ransom note.

That made no sense. According to Nan, it

was virtually worthless now because it was incomplete.

Where was the kit now? I looked at the picture again. It had been photographed on this desk. I opened all the drawers, even the ones I knew were too small to hold the box.

I tried the closet door. It was locked. I grabbed the key off the fabric and inserted it, pulling the door open hard. I stuck the key in my pocket. I expected to see the two sewing kits, side by side on the floor, but the closet was empty.

I heard the lunch bell ring, and the chatter of quilters as they passed on their way to the dining hall. I thought of Nan, mournfully playing the piano this morning. She'd been so sad. For a moment, I'd thought I could have given her some good news.

Where was Mercedes?

I walked outside, frustrated, and ran down the stone steps. There was one sleeping room below the main level. Through the window, I saw Mercedes' distinctive pink briefcase. Rather than leave her stuff in the open living room, she must have locked up her work stuff in her room before going to lunch. The sewing box could be inside.

I stepped down until I was at the door to the room and knocked loudly. When there was no answer, I tried the knob.

Locked, of course. I peered into the window alongside the door. I could see a desk with a pink file and a laptop. No sewing boxes.

The curtain blew against the open window. The window was low to the ground and wide enough for me to crawl in. The ledge came right to my hip. If I could get the screen off, I could get in. Building in a more genteel era, the architect had not anticipated burglars. People were far more trusting in those days, not expecting people to crawl in through the windows.

I looked around. This side of the building faced away from the main lodge and away from the dining hall. Behind me was a wooded slope. If I moved quickly, I could get in and out before anyone knew I was there.

I pulled at the screen's wooden frame. It moved slightly. I broke a nail, trying to pry it away from the window. A car key would help. Or a nail file. I wasn't the type to go for acrylic nails that could be used as a tool. Too bad my keys were locked up.

I tried using the skeleton key in my pocket. I got in under the track. The screen popped off and I shoved the window open wider. It stuck slightly in the track, but then gave way. I crawled over the sill, landing awkwardly on the desk chair. I stepped down and pulled the curtain closed so that no passersby would see me.

No sewing boxes in sight. This room had a closet, too. I pulled on the knob, but it wouldn't give. Another locked door.

Skeleton keys would fit most any lock. I tried the one from upstairs. The door knob turned with a satisfying click.

There it was. The Rose Box was on the floor of the closet. I peered into the space behind it, expecting to see the German Cross box, too, but only the Rose Box was there. I opened it. The slot for the sewing bird was still empty.

I closed the door, making sure the lock didn't engage. I wanted to be able to access the space again.

What to do? If I confronted Mercedes alone, she might train her gun on me. Fake or no, the fact was that she'd been willing to pull it on Paul. I didn't want to chance her having a real one nearby.

I could find the gun and take it with me, but there wasn't enough time to do that and get Tony here before lunch was over.

I thought about moving the box to a spot where it could be seen from the outside. But if I did that and Mercedes returned before I did, I was screwed.

A pretty pink paisley box marked "Vehicles" sat on the desk. I opened the lid and found my set of car keys. I'd be able to get around so much faster in my car.

I made sure the door to the outside didn't lock automatically. I needed to be able to tell Tony that I'd found the room open. I crossed my fingers that Mercedes was busy with dietary problems in the dining hall and wouldn't return to her room early.

I used the house phone on the outside wall to call the Ranger station. Tony was out to lunch, the friendly voice said. In town; she wasn't sure where.

I cruised slowly down Lighthouse Avenue. I looked again at the picture I'd found in the living room. Tony would be interested to know that Mercedes had been blackmailing someone. The Rose Box wasn't valuable without the sewing bird. Mercedes — or whoever she'd sent the picture to — had to have the missing tool.

Nan had been right about one thing: the second box had been stolen to cover for the real theft. The object of desire was not the German Cross Box, but the Rose.

I got to the end without seeing him or his car. I made a U-turn by the theater and headed back toward Asilomar.

My mind was reeling. What was I going to

do now?

One of the last commercial buildings on the way out of town was a small red house. Diners sat on the patio. I slowed, trying to spot my brother.

Tony was alone, leaning against a post. I parked along the side street, and waved him over. He lumbered off the porch. I never would have looked for him here. It was a cute little gem of a victorian house, converted to a lunch place — very "ladies who lunch." Not rangers who munch.

I called to him, "Tony, come with me."

He opened the passenger door, glancing up the street. "Sis, I'm waiting for someone . . ."

"Please. Get in, there's no time to waste. Lunch hour's nearly over."

He gave a glance at his watch and again at the street. He clearly had an appointment.

I begged him again. "It's got to do with the troubles at Sewing-by-the-Sea. It's important."

He got in, and I pulled out, barely giving him time to close his door. He pulled his seat belt around him.

"What's going on?" he said, texting as he talked. I tried to peek, but beyond, "Duty calls," I couldn't see any more of the message.

"Did you hear about the stolen sewing box?" I asked.

He nodded. "Mercedes reported it to us, yes."

"It's no longer missing. I saw it in Mercedes' room. We've got to get back before she's finished with lunch."

"Dewey, slow down." I glanced at my speedometer. I was doing forty-five in a twenty-five zone. I took my foot off the gas.

"This is serious, Tony. Mercedes was threatening to sue the Park Service for not securing the building." It was only a little lie. She'd sue if she could.

Now I had his full attention. "And this thing is in her room?"

"In the Pirates' Den. Her room."

Tony looked at me suspiciously. "How do you know?"

I lied smoothly. When my brother'd left home for college, I was just honing my dissembling skills. He didn't know how good I was. "I went by to see Mercedes and I saw it. Sitting in a closet." I hadn't thought up a good cover story, and I was faltering, but Tony didn't seem to notice.

"Maybe she's returning it to the owner."

We were pulling into Asilomar. I parked in a fifteen-minute spot reserved for registering guests because it was closer to the

Pirates' Den. I'd have to take the chance that Mercedes might see my car. But being in violation of her no-keys rule was nothing compared to stealing Nan's sewing kit.

I was ready to burst through the door, but Tony stopped me a few feet away from it. He knocked loudly. "Miss Madsen?" he said.

"Sis," he said. "I can't just waltz in here."

"Look in the window," I urged. Maybe he'd see the case, though I knew it was hopeless. I'd left the case in the closet and closed the door.

He protested, but pressed his face against the screen. "I would need cause to open . . ."

He stopped and straightened. His eyes went flat and he grabbed the gun at his belt.

"What?" I said, my heart flipping over at the sight of my brother in law enforcement mode.

"Stand back," he said.

I took a step forward.

"Dewey," he warned, his voice harsh. I'd never heard that particular tone from him before. I backed up, across the sidewalk and against the retaining wall.

He spoke into this walkie-talkie, a series of codes I didn't understand.

"Now what?" I said as he stood guarding the door, eyes roaming the area without lighting on me or anything else for long.

"You wait here. Don't move."

He opened the door.

I paced outside. It was close to one o'clock. Soon three hundred quilters, including Mercedes, would leave the dining hall and start back to class. Someone was bound to pass. Mercedes was inevitably on her way here. My heart hammered.

Tony's walkie-talkie crackled inside and he shut the door firmly. I forced myself to be calm. I cracked my knuckles, channeling Vangie at the height of the tension. I didn't get the same relief she did.

I tried to focus on the outcome. It would be nice to see Nan's face when the sewing kit was returned to her. She would be so happy.

The door opened a crack. "Dewey, you need to stand way back."

My foot, which had been inching toward him, stopped dead. "What is it, Tony?"

His face was in shadow. A gull's plaintive cry split the air. "When you were here earlier, the room was empty?"

"Yes, completely."

"You weren't in here, right?"

I felt a pit open in my stomach. I'd already told him I hadn't been in. I couldn't get him in that kind of trouble. A sister who breaks and enters.

"Of course not," I said with as much bluster as I could. "I told you I just looked in the window. Why?"

Tony came out, closing the door behind him. His face was grave. He rubbed at his nose, and pulled on his lower lip. A scenario came rushing back at me. Tony at eighteen, having wrecked the family van. He'd been tugging on his lip while Dad lectured him about the finer points of driving in the first rain of the season.

"She's dead, Dewey. Mercedes is lying on the floor. Deceased."

FIFTEEN

"Are you messing with me? Because if this is your idea of a joke," I said, moving toward Tony, trying to get past him.

He came out, blood on the hem of his khakis. He must have taken her pulse. "This is a crime scene. I've got to establish a perimeter. You are a civilian. Stand back."

A crime scene. Murder? I could believe she'd died of a heart attack or an aneurysm, but that didn't mean crime scene. A crime scene I'd been a part of.

I inspected the window I'd opened earlier. There was no evidence that anyone had broken in. My heart rate slowed a bit.

I looked at the frame, but there was no sign that the door had been forced. No gouge marks, no scratches on the lock. The hinges were intact. Mercedes had opened the door to her attacker.

She had let someone in with the ultimate complaint.

As Tony opened the door wide enough to slip back into the room, I took a look inside.

The closet door was open. I was betting the missing sewing kit was gone again, but I didn't ask about that.

"Did you find her gun?"

"Her gun?" Tony said seriously. He creased his forehead.

"Earlier in the week, she pointed it at Paul Wiggins."

"Paul Wiggins, the guy whose wife went into the ocean?" Tony was confused, and I knew he wouldn't stop until he had everything straight in his mind. It was very important to him that things match up.

I explained, "Paul tried to get on campus the other day. He thought his wife was here. Mercedes took umbrage at his demands, and produced a gun to drive him away."

"Why didn't you tell me?" Tony asked.

"She told me it wasn't real."

"The gun that killed her was real," he said.

So she'd been shot. Poor Mercedes.

Tony was scowling. I felt the twinge of being a six-year-old getting in her big brother's way as he was leaving for school.

"Are you sure that you saw the sewing box?" he said. "I mean, you were outside looking in, right? You could have been mistaken."

"It was in there," I said. "The killer must have taken it."

"That's not the only plausible scenario. Her assistant could have removed it. The owner could have stopped by and gotten it. There could be any number of reasons why it's no longer in the room. We can't jump to conclusions."

You can't jump to conclusions, I thought. I could jump any old way I wanted to.

"I bet Paul killed her," I said.

"Dewey, come on. Leave this to the experts."

I bristled. "Look, Tony, I've probably taken part in more homicides than you have. I'm not a suspect here. I did not touch the gun."

"And you never went into the room?" he said, watching my face closely. I tightened my lips, keeping my face neutral. I didn't want him reading my expression.

I was saved from answering by the appearance of Ranger Schmitt, followed quickly by Detective Graham of Pacific Grove PD. I was shunted outside as the police entered the room and took over the crime scene.

I found a rock to sit on. I could see the ocean from here, and vaguely hear the sea lions on Seal Rock screaming their names.

A car from the Attorney General's office

arrived. Soon after, the Monterey County Coroner. The police gathered in the lot below. The death investigation had begun.

I thought about what I'd seen. The missing sewing kit was there and then gone again. What did that mean? Mercedes had taken it from the chapel. Why? Or had she found it?

I needed to talk to Nan, the sewing tool expert. Had Mercedes told her that she'd found the kit? I wasn't looking forward to telling her that the box had disappeared again. She'd looked miserable about it the first time. How many times can a heart break before it's irreparable?

I found the officer in charge and asked permission to leave.

"Give me your cell number," he said.

That was a wrinkle. "Sorry, I don't have it. Ms. Madsen, the dead woman, insisted on collecting our cells at the beginning of the week. It's probably in there," I said, nodding my head toward Mercedes' room. Part of the sealed crime scene.

He made a note. "How can I reach you?"

Tony stepped forward. "This is my sister, Officer Graham. I'll make myself available to contact her whenever you need her."

"I'm staying at Asilomar for the rest of the week," I said. I gave him a QP business card. "After that, you can get me here."

"You didn't enter the room when Ranger Pellicano did?" he said.

I shook my head earnestly. Well, I didn't.

"All right," he said. "I'll be in touch."

I had to stop myself from running away. I couldn't wait to be out of there. I would leave the detecting to the professionals. I just wanted to know about the sewing kit and how it related back to Ursula Wiggins. Or the Ghost.

I didn't stick around to see Mercedes' body being removed.

Where would Nan be? I tried to remember what class she'd said she was in, but I couldn't. I'd have to check all the classrooms or wait for dinner.

As I passed the bike rack outside the Administration building, I saw the pay phone. For the first time in days, I was free to call Buster without interference. I fed coins to the phone eagerly.

He didn't answer. Probably still in court. I felt the disappointment like a blow to the gut. My eyes filled with tears. I really wanted to tell him what had just happened. I shook myself, trying to escape the feelings that Mercedes' death was dragging up in me. Feelings of dread, of waste, of the pain we humans inflicted on each other. Buster could always help me put things in perspective.

I walked through the Asilomar grounds, peeking into classrooms, trying to catch sight of Nan.

If Mercedes took the Rose Box, what had she done with the German Cross box? Maybe she ransomed that one off already. To Harriet. How much would Harriet pay to get that abomination out of circulation?

I knew where Harriet was. In Legendary Quilts. I started to go back to my class.

I looked into the buildings as I walked, trying to see if I could spot Nan's head among the students.

I pulled open the door to Evergreen, where my class was being held. Cinnamon nodded to me. I mouthed an apology. She smiled. But Harriet was not in the room.

I asked Lucy as I sat down, "Did Harriet come back after lunch?"

She shook her head. "She went to lie down before we ate. Said she had a massive headache."

Lucy was excited about something else. She showed me pictures she'd found. "My grandfather was an original Pirate," she said proudly. "You know, the first men that lived here at Asilomar. Carlos let me borrow these pictures from the dining hall. I have to have them back before dinner."

I recognized the black and white shots of Asilomar interiors. Many of these were the places I'd been photographing earlier. The white writing identified Lucy's grandfather as one of the grinning young men dressed in white T-shirts and jeans.

"He looks very rakish," I said.

Lucy smiled. "Not exactly the man I knew."

"Isn't it fun?" I asked. "To get to know him as an unattached guy?"

Lucy concurred. Cinnamon asked for our attention. I was stuck in class for the afternoon. I'd already missed so much of the class, I couldn't walk out again.

"Let your ideas percolate," Cinnamon said. "Without looking at the pictures you've taken, continue sewing. Let the mindless rhythm of the machine free your mind. You'll be amazed at the connections you make."

My mind swirled as I sewed, but instead of seeing the pictures of the buildings I'd taken, I was getting images of Mercedes, Ursula's cape, the sewing boxes. I fed bits of fabric under the presser foot and let my mind wander.

Why did Ursula make the trek to Asilomar just to end her life? According to Paul, she came here every year. According to Mercedes, she'd stopped coming years ago. Who was right?

I didn't come up with any answers. Only more questions.

As soon as the dinner bell rang, I ran over to the dining hall. I positioned myself on the broad outdoor steps, right next to the menu board, so I could see everyone who entered. I would catch Nan or Harriet, whoever came first.

Red came up the steps. I saw Freddy and Quentin approaching.

"Coming in?" she said to me.

"In a minute," I said.

"I'll save you a seat."

She looked at Freddy and Quentin as they caught up with her. "If it isn't the Double-mint Twins. Are you two a couple, or what?"

Freddy looked dismayed, as though his innate heterosexuality should be evident beneath his groomed nails and purple polyester.

I heard him recounting the number of girlfriends he had as they entered. Quentin was chuckling.

I kept watching. After a few minutes of solid traffic, only a few stragglers remained. I was surprised to see several rangers, including my brother, gathering. They were solemn. Tony nodded at me, but his face was grim.

"We need everyone inside," said the oldest ranger, tall and thin, with distinguished gray temples. His badge said Ranger Kirby. His authority was unmistakable.

I obeyed and found a seat near Sherry and Red. Freddy joined us. I saw Nan across the room. She must have gotten here before I did. I wanted to ask about Harriet, but Ranger Kirby held up his hand to get our attention.

Tony and the other rangers, men and women, stood at parade rest, their hands clasped behind their backs.

"I'm sorry to inform you that the body of your conference leader, Mercedes Madsen, has been found."

"The *body?*" a woman hissed next to me.

"Sssh," Red said. She was joined by others in the room, effectively silencing everyone into stunned acquiescence.

I was thinking how grateful I was that I hadn't been the one to find Mercedes. Another body. I'd seen more than my share in the last year. Too many dead people.

The ranger continued, "There has never before been a shooting death at Asilomar. We take our duties very seriously. We will be assisted in the investigation by the Pacific Grove Police, and the Monterey County Sheriff's department."

I heard the whispering start up again.

"Shooting?"

"She was murdered . . ." someone said.

"We want to talk to anyone who has information about Ms. Madsen's whereabouts today. We will be using the ranger station as our command central. We will be conducting interviews there. Before you leave here, you must give us your contact information and set up an appointment to talk with law enforcement."

I looked at my brother. I hadn't thought of the Rangers as a military organization, but it was quite clear now. Tony's face was blank.

The ranger continued, "We can assure you that you are safe here. We've assigned more ranger patrols. We are at your disposal. We want to make sure the rest of your week is as successful as the first half. To that end, we hope you will remain on-site."

The rangers filed out.

I caught up to Tony.

"Have the police talked with Paul Wiggins?" I asked.

Tony waited for the other rangers to disperse before he asked, "Why?"

"I told you. He had a big fight with Mercedes the day before."

"The police have probably had a word with him."

"You have to make sure, Tony. He hated Mercedes. If you could have seen the two of them together . . ."

"Whoa, girl. I'm not about to tell the police how to do their job. And I suggest you stay clear of it."

"What about the gun?"

"What about it?" Tony asked, clearly wanting to move on.

I persisted, "Did you find the fake gun in Mercedes' room? It should have been there."

He was shaking his head. "How big was this gun, Dewey?"

"Small. Tiny, no bigger than the palm of my hand."

"Mercedes was killed with a small caliber bullet, but the weapon hasn't been recovered. I've got to go, Dewey."

I wandered back to my table. The room was abuzz with chatter.

The door to the dining hall was swept open dramatically. A woman strode up the middle aisle, wearing a colorful scarf wrapped around her head. She was wearing zebra-striped sandals and a black linen pant-suit.

My stomach tightened. I knew that walk. Oh no, it wasn't. It couldn't be.

She slowed, as if she was in slow-motion instant replay, so I could get a better look. I couldn't see her face, but that stride was too familiar.

I felt an elbow in my ribs. Freddy was nudging me, pointing with his right hand, his manicured nail catching the low light. He turned to me, his face filled with glee. Freddy liked nothing better than trouble, and this was trouble.

My jaw had dropped open. Freddy used his finger to close my mouth.

"That is so not a good look for her," he said disapproving, using his finger to pro-scribe a circle in the air that took in her covered head.

"Isn't that your —" Sherry asked.

"Who?" Quentin asked. He craned his neck, trying to see over the heads of the quilters in front of him. "Who is it?"

I steadied myself on the table. The salad on the Lazy Susan smelled like fennel. The odor was acting like smelling salts, going straight to my head.

"Let the fun begin," Freddy said, clapping

195

his hands joyously.

The woman in the headscarf was Kym.

Sixteen

"What has she done, converted to Islam?" Freddy said. "She's practically wearing a burka."

I didn't keep up with Kevin and Kym's religious choices, but I was pretty sure I would have heard about that.

"No," I hissed. "Shut up and listen."

"Kym who?" Quentin asked.

Kym spoke, her face still only partially visible. "Please pardon my appearance. I've been suffering from an allergic reaction to a doctor-ordered skin treatment."

Freddy squealed, "She's had Botox and it went wrong. That guy injected beef fat into her skin. Or squirrel lard."

I jammed my elbow in his side, this time like I meant to hurt him. "Shut up."

"It could be a bad face peel," Quentin put in. "If she went into the sun after a chemical peel, she would blow up like a balloon."

I gave them both what I hoped was a

withering look. Red and Sherry exchanged a glance. Freddy squashed a giggle.

Kym's scarf slipped. From here, her face looked like a boiled beet. Kym looked panicked. I knew that look. She was afraid no one was listening to her. Pretty soon, she would get nasty because she felt stupid. I didn't want to be around for that. I'd too often been the target of her tirades.

What was she doing here? This was Mini-Mer? The fabulous assistant that Mercedes had bragged about? I couldn't imagine Kym organizing a conference of this magnitude, with international teachers and hundreds of students.

I had a lot of questions. But I wasn't holding my breath for the answers. I was the last person she'd confide in.

Too bad I couldn't call Jenn. My employee, Jenn, had been Kym's best friend at QP. How much of this had Jenn known? Had she known Kym would be here? I was pretty sure she knew all of it, but hadn't told me out of loyalty to Kym.

Kym looked everywhere, except in my direction. She cleared her throat several times, and poked a finger under her scarf, scratching. She caught herself, and held both hands in front of her, hanging on tightly.

"I'm so sorry —" she stopped, caught her breath. Her boss was dead.

She gathered herself, and started again. "I am Kym Pellicano."

At the mention of her name, Red gave me a funny look.

"I work for Sewing-by-the-Sea. With Mercedes gone —" she choked on the word, but kept going. "I'm in charge."

She seemed to gain strength as the audience remained focused on her. "You've heard the Rangers guarantee your safety. We have two days remaining in the Sewing-by-the-Sea Symposium. I want, as I know Mercedes would have, for you to get the most out of your classes. I have met with your teachers, and they are willing to complete the coursework. Mercedes would have wanted the seminar to go on despite her early demise."

The crowd murmured, but there were no protests. I got the feeling that most of them were grateful to have the decision made for them. They'd come here to sew. Many had taken time off work, and arranged for care for grandkids or husbands, paid for airline tickets. A collective sigh of relief went up.

Kym had paused, waiting for the talk to cease. When she spoke again, her voice was soft, filled with regret. "If you have any questions, I will be running things from Pirates' Den living room. Come find me anytime."

The murmurs got louder, and Kym fought to maintain control of the crowd.

She raised her voice. "Finish your meal," she said. "Tonight's lecture by Australian teacher, Judy Sherlock, will begin at seven in the chapel. I encourage you to attend. Judy has traveled a long distance and has gone to a lot of trouble to be here for you."

"This is turning out to be quite the week," Freddy said, ticking off his fingers for emphasis. "First, an unknown lady falls into the sea. Second, two prized sewing boxes are taken, and now Mercedes murdered. Awesome."

"Did you know Ursula?" I asked. I didn't realize he knew about her.

"Who?" he asked.

"Never mind." Freddy just collected bad events. He didn't really care about the people involved.

I saw Kym sit down and pick at the food she was given. I kept an eye on her, wanting to waylay her as soon as she left. I wanted to talk to Buster, and I needed Kym to give me my cell.

I saw her get up and leave, alone.

"Kym!" I called. My sister-in-law was a

few feet ahead of me, working her way down the stone steps to the asphalt drive below.

She stopped and I heard her let out a tortured breath. Obviously, she knew who was calling her name.

"Dewey," she said, scratching her cheek under her scarf. "I don't have a lot of time to chat. I have arrangements to make for Mercedes. I'm coordinating with her family in Oakland. Her husband and son are on their way."

"I don't care about Mercedes," I said, regretting how harsh it sounded when I heard Kym's intake of breath. She moved away from me. I could smell the salt air and tried to take its curative powers in.

"Wait," I said. "That came out wrong. I meant I don't want to keep you from your duties, I just need my phone back."

I caught up to her. She didn't look at me. Her face was mostly in shadow, covered by the retro print scarf, but I could see ugly red welts on her forehead and cheeks.

"What's up with your face?" I asked.

"Allergies."

We walked uphill, Kym's wheezing growing worse as we went. "Are you sure you're okay?" I asked.

"I can't breathe. I just need my inhaler. It's back at the room. Whatever I'm allergic to has affected my lungs."

Dramatic Kym. She never had handled being sick very well. Every itch was fatal, every pimple an abscess, every sniffle a symptom of a pandemic.

"As long as you're here, you can turn your car keys back in."

How did she know? "My keys?"

"I saw you driving earlier. Just hand them over." She held out her palm imperiously. She seemed to have learned from Mercedes.

"I had to drive to get Tony. He's the one who found Mercedes."

She flinched slightly. "I know. He told me Mercedes was dead," she said.

"What do you think about her murder?"

"I can't think about that. If I'm going to make a go of these seminars, I have to make sure this one finishes without any more hitches."

A murder was a little more than a hitch.

"What do you know?" I asked, alert to the fear in her voice. Kym knew something about Mercedes. "Was she into illegal doings?"

Kym shut down. "As if I'm going to talk to you about Mercedes. I've told the police everything they need to know."

"Is Kevin coming down to help you?" I

asked. My little brother was probably already on his way.

To my surprise, she shook her head. Her scarf slipped and she adjusted it, tying it tighter around her neck.

"He can't get away. They're behind schedule so he has to stay on his job site."

Her delivery was flat. It had to be killing her that Kevin couldn't be here in her time of crisis.

"So this is your new job?" I asked.

"Yes," Kym said with a defiant scowl. "I love it."

"How's this going to work?" I asked. Kevin worked for my father's construction business, based in San Jose. If Kym was going to take over Mercedes' seminars, she'd have to be down here in Monterey six or seven weeks out of the year. She'd never before wanted to be apart from my brother. Was there trouble in paradise?

Kym's mouth was set in a straight line, as though she was afraid to talk. She and I had never had a close relationship, but I'd had faint hopes that once she'd stopped working at Quilter Paradiso, she would become friendly. Instead, she'd gotten more distant.

Kym and I were farther apart than ever now. We had barely spoken in the last couple of months. I had no idea where she and

Kevin were in their lives. Indeed, they could have converted to Islam. Or moved to Pacific Grove.

My firing her had made the men in my family react in weird ways. My dad stopped his Sunday Suppers, sick of me not wanting to attend if Kym was coming, and vice versa. Kevin and Buster went to the park to shoot hoops without me. Just when Kevin and I had been getting closer, firing Kym had driven a nail between us.

Tony had never fallen for the family drama. I could trust him to hear my side. Kym had no hold on him.

We entered the Pirates' Den. From this side, I couldn't see the police activity below.

"So, can I have my cell?" I said, reasonably.

"No phones is Sewing-by-the-Sea policy."

"Hold on," I said. "You're not serious. Mercedes is no longer here. You can give us ours back now."

"The ban on phones was not just Mercedes' decision. The students objected to the number of times classes were interrupted. At their suggestion, it is how we do things at Sewing-by-the-Sea. I am upholding that policy."

"Besides," she said. "The phones were secured in Mercedes' room. Mercedes put everything of value in her room so it could be locked up tight."

Behind crime scene tape, in other words. I'd figured they were being held in the Pirates' Den. I should have realized it stood to reason the keys and the cell phones had been locked in her room.

I sighed.

"I'm going to the lecture now," Kym said. "I've got to introduce Judy."

She gathered up her things and we headed out the door. Her next question startled me.

"What are you going to do about Tony?" she asked.

I took a step back, and cocked an eyebrow. "What do you mean?"

"Come on, Dewey, don't be like that. There is no reason to pretend you don't know he's moved back here to be near someone special."

"I have no idea what you're talking about."

My own questions about Tony came back to me. Why had he missed our coffee date? Who was he supposed to meet for lunch today?

I felt the uncertainty gnaw at my stomach. Damn. Oh, how I hated being in the position of Kym knowing more than me. It really grinded me. I stopped and took a breath.

"Did you ever wonder why he's in Monterey?" she said.

"Oh, that." This was a no-brainer. "He told me he works patrol over there. That's part of his area."

"I don't think historical Monterey is all he's patrolling. I'm just saying," she said, shrugging daintily. She looked oddly unbalanced without her customary hair toss. The scarf was making it harder for her to communicate.

"Tony would have told me if he had a girlfriend," I insisted.

"Okay, whatever. I get it. He's your brother. Just don't forget, he's Kevin's brother, too."

Tony confides in Kevin. And Kevin confides in Kym. That doesn't include me.

I tried nonchalance. "If she exists, I'm sure he'll introduce me as soon as he's ready."

I presumed Tony had had women over the years, but he'd never brought anyone home to meet the family. No one special enough. If this girl was important enough that he'd mentioned her to Kevin, the relationship could be really special. I fought down the urge to be jealous of Kym with the urge to be happy for my brother.

Kym started toward Merrill Hall. I turned

on my heel and went in the opposite direction. I walked down the steps that led to Mercedes' room. The door was open. A Pacific Grove policeman was standing guard. He was beefy and looked very little older than the average mall cop.

"How's it going?" I asked, trying to peer past him into her room. It was far messier than when I'd been inside. Two armchairs were overturned, and I could see Mercedes' careful piles of paper strewn on the floor. There had definitely been a fight in that room. Mercedes had not gone to her demise easily.

The cop's cell rang and he took a step away. I heard him talking about the logistics of childcare for his two-year-old now that he wasn't getting home on time so I moved closer to the open door. The room was bright. The overhead lights that made it impossible to read in bed lit the room with no shadows.

Something had broken — there were shards of glass on the floor. The curtain on the one window was torn down as though someone had grabbed onto them.

Had someone been looking for something in Mercedes' papers? Addresses or phone numbers? Maybe it had nothing to do with the sewing box. Credit card information might be valuable enough to kill.

Except the sewing box was gone.

The young policeman was pleading with his wife. He'd evidently reneged on too many promises to cook dinner and watch the baby. He gestured for me to move on.

I went back up to the living room. I'd laid my blueprint fabric down and needed to retrieve it.

A woman was standing by the window that overlooked where the policeman was pacing. Her back was to me. She'd opened the window and was leaning on the table in front of it, trying to see out.

I couldn't see her face and she didn't hear me approach. She shifted, trying to get a better angle to see what was going on. Her face appeared in the mirror on the wall to her left, just over the desk.

Her profile was familiar.

Fading sunlight came in through the window, offering me the red highlights in her hair. I knew then where I'd seen her. Her hair was short now, but it was the same color. This was the woman I saw go off the cliff three days ago.

I gasped. She turned, and her own breath stuttered.

Her face darkened. She looked like a trapped animal. She tried to leave, but I

208

blocked the door.

"It was you," I managed to squeak out. My lungs felt empty and no air was coming in. Beneath the noise of the investigation downstairs, I could hear the ocean.

"You died," I said. "You jumped into the water."

"I fooled you, did I?" she said, her smile growing broader and yet sadder. Her eyes drifted to the door behind me. She was trapped. "Allow me to introduce myself. I'm Ursula Wiggins."

"I know who you are," I said, angrily. "You're the woman who died right before me. How dare you?"

"How dare I what? Die? I've wanted to die for so long. Dying would have been welcome. But the human spirit isn't easily snuffed out. My husband tried. Lord, how he tried."

I felt anger at her. I knew she was the victim, but she acted so damn weak. "You could have gotten help."

Her eyes flashed. "We're no longer in fashion, battered women. Not a cause célèbre. No more TV movies, or Oprah appearances. No one wants to know about us."

I made a disgusted sound.

"You have no idea," she shouted.

I stood up to her. "I've met murderers

face-to-face. I've been in danger. I know what it is like."

Her eyes narrowed. "You're a naïve little girl. Your ignorance is dangerous because you think you've seen evil, you think you know what evil is. You've never met anyone who exists only to hurt you."

I was silent. The force of her words was like a hammer, striking my core. I opened my mouth again, but she held up a restraining hand.

"Consider this. The one person on earth who's meant to love you. The real you, the grownup you. That person turns on you, using love as an excuse to kill you slowly. What you saw, that woman who went off the cliff, she's been dead for a long time. Starting on her honeymoon, thirty years ago."

"You had no right to involve me," I said, my ire dissipating — but I still needed to be heard. "I thought I could have stopped you and then you were dead."

She backed up toward the fireplace. It had been swept clean and a new fire laid.

"I had no choice. What you saw was a mercy killing, the only way I could exist. I have a right to a life, too. And I had to take extreme measures to get there. Birth is painful. Rebirth, even more painful. You weren't a witness to a death, you were a witness to a birth, bloody and full of hurt."

I felt the steam going out of my argument. As much as I'd been hurt by thinking I'd seen a suicide, I hadn't suffered for decades at the hands of a psychopath. One that lived in my house, ate the meals I cooked, and left the toilet seat up.

"How did you do it?" I said.

Her eyes strayed to the door behind me. I went over and turned the lock so no one else could come in, and pulled the curtains shut.

"You owe me a true explanation," I said. "I told the rangers that you'd died. I started a huge rescue mission. I'm going to look like an idiot now. Sit down and tell me how you pulled this off."

She didn't sit. She paced in front of the fireplace, unconsciously acting out her words. "I dropped my cape. I hated to give up that cape. I walked into the water. It was so cold, my ankles went numb. I hid behind a rock until you went for help. Then I ran to my car, using the rocks as a shield. You almost caught me several times."

I remembered the van I'd seen drive by. "The VW?" I said.

She nodded. "Rent-a-Wreck."

Another thought occurred to me. "Are

211

you the Ghost? Don't you have a boyfriend here?"

She laughed. "A boyfriend? Hell, no. There's no way I want anything to do with men."

I could understand that. "But you are the Ghost?"

She nodded. "I didn't plan to go missing every year. I wanted to go to Sewing-by-the-Sea like everyone else. To learn more about quilting. But the first year I came, Paul had beaten me the night before I got on the plane. Nothing that showed, mind you, but my ribs were broken, my teeth were nearly out of my head. I went to the morning session, miserable and in terrible pain. After that, I crawled back to bed and stayed there. I could barely move."

She drew back into the chair. "Paul knew it looked good to our friends if he allowed me to come to this week-long seminar. What a great husband, the girls at the quilt shop would say, he even pays for her to have a private room."

She gave a bitter laugh. "So every year, he'd send me off. But first, he would give me his private send-off. I could barely sit on the plane, and most of the time I couldn't sit all day in a class, so I just stayed in my room."

"The second or third year, Mercedes tracked me down. She came to my room, trying to force me to go to class. But I explained the situation to her, and she was sympathetic. Turned out her mother was abused by her stepfather."

"So you worked out a deal with her. Paul would pay for the registration and Mercedes would kick something back to you."

"Enough for me to live on my own for a week."

Ursula's voice broke. She held herself so still, like an animal who didn't want to be seen. "She told me she would help me if I ever decided to leave. She'd get me a fake ID and money. This year was the year. I'm getting free."

I didn't know what else to say. She had a right to her freedom.

Finally she looked at me and said, her voice low and tight. "You can't tell anyone where I am. You can't lead my husband to me."

"I won't tell him," I said. "But the police? They're looking for you."

She shook her head. Her short hair suited her, giving her face a lift. Or maybe it was the start of her new life.

"They're not. They're waiting for my body to wash up on shore."

I couldn't deny that.

"Once Mercedes gives me what I'm owed, you'll never see me again, I promise."

Mercedes? She didn't know. "Mercedes is gone, Ursula."

"What do you mean?" she said.

"Mercedes was shot. Right below us. In her room."

"Shot? But I just saw her." Ursula's face drained of color. The large age spot on her cheek seemed to throb.

"What do you mean, you just saw her?" I asked.

Ursula's hand went to her mouth. "How am I going to get out of here now?"

I stood. "I'll help you. My brother is a ranger here. We can get you out."

"No!" she yelled.

I wasn't expecting her to come at me with the poker, but she did. Hard enough to knock me out.

Seventeen

My head throbbed. I came to on the floor. Alone. I wasn't sure how much time had passed, but it was dark out.

I got my legs under me and tried to stand. I could only get as far as my knees. My head was spinning like I'd drunk a six-pack of Coors. Underneath was a pounding, relentless as the surf.

I put my hand up to my forehead, fully expecting to see blood when I took it away, but my fingers were clean. Nothing felt sticky. She hadn't broken the skin, just conked me hard and put me down long enough for her to get away.

I would have a knot on my head, but it didn't seem serious. I'd had a concussion in high school, the result of an ill-timed kick to the head in a soccer match. This didn't feel like that.

Holding my head with both hands, I stood a little taller. I leaned into the armchair, letting its bulk hold me up. I took a couple of quick, energizing breaths. My head still hurt, but the feeling of being underwater was fading.

I couldn't let myself give in to the pain. I picked up my head, waiting for the dizziness to pass. I had to find Ursula.

I unlocked the door and went outside, trying to orient myself. I walked down the hill to the parking lot. The Sand and Sea classroom was dark, so it had to be after midnight. There was no way I was going to find her.

Ursula was long gone.

I stood in the parking lot. The cops were gone. No one was around. I heard an owl. I didn't feel wise. At all.

I knew I shouldn't let myself sleep, but I was so tired, it was all I could do to stumble to my room.

I was alive the next morning. I knew, because my head was pounding. I painfully pulled my hair back and leaned into the mirror. I could see a reddened spot just north of my forehead that felt slightly raised. My hair would cover it. I brushed my hair over it, careful not to touch the bristles to the sore. I downed four aspirin and vowed not to move too quickly.

It was early, but I needed to talk to Buster, so I got dressed and walked over to the Administration building. I zipped my Neoprene jacket. The morning air was cool.

I used the pay phone to call Buster. I could tell I'd awakened him. He sounded sleepy. And sexy, his voice gravelly from not being used yet.

"Hey," he said, when he heard my voice.

"You in bed?" I asked. I could be there in a little more than an hour. All I had to do was pack up my stuff and drive home. Get under the sheets with Buster and stay there. It would be warm and I'd have Buster's bulk to comfort me.

"What are you doing up so early?" he said.

The reason I'd called him came back to me in a rush. "There's been a murder, Buster."

He didn't ask me if I was kidding. He knew I wouldn't tease him about something like that.

"Are you okay?"

His first thought was about me. This guy was the best. I cupped the phone, trying to transmit some of the love I felt for him through the wires.

"I'm okay."

"Tell me what happened," he said.

I heard him shifting, sitting up. A pen

217

clicked. He'd be taking notes even though it wasn't his case.

"I found Mercedes Madsen dead in her room. Well, Tony did. But I was right outside."

"Mercedes, the warden?" he asked.

"Yes, the conference coordinator. The one who ripped the phone out of my hand the other night."

"She probably made a lot of enemies acting like that."

"Believe it or not, everyone loved her."

He grunted. "How did she die?"

"She'd been shot."

"Didn't anyone hear anything?"

"Everyone was at lunch," I said.

"Not everyone," Buster said grimly. "The police are there?"

"Yes. Do you know any of the Pacific Grove police?" I asked. I might need to ask some questions.

"Not really. I might know one or two in the Monterey Sheriff's department. We had a training day at Asilomar last year and I met a couple of homicide guys there."

"I'd like to know their theory of the crime," I said.

"What do *you* think happened?" he asked.

I could talk to Buster. He would let me give my opinions, he trusted me to tell him the truth. At least as far as I saw it.

But standing outside of the Administration building, even as early as it was, I didn't want to say much. Anyone could overhear. Paul Wiggins might be lurking.

"Any chance you can come down?" I said. I heard the bed creak as he stood up. He was probably wearing his favorite boxers, white and blue pin-striped. Or maybe his SF Giants Jockey shorts. I could practically smell the musky heat coming off his neck.

I whined, "It's Wednesday. You promised."

He sighed. "I'm still on the stand. The defense has been dragging their heels, asking me dopey questions. Trying to question my methodology. The prosecutor objects a lot and the lawyers and the judge head into chambers and before you know it, another morning has gone by."

"I miss you," I said.

"I'll be there as soon as I can. They promised me I'd be done soon. I'll get in my car as soon as I'm wrapped up."

I hung up the phone, wondering what to do next. It was too early for breakfast. From the other side of the building, I could hear the surf. The morning darkness was beginning to let up. I walked through the Administration building. One person was on duty at the desk and nodded at me. Otherwise, the place was deserted.

I came out the other side, taking in a deep breath, letting the sea air in.

The sun had risen further, giving the air a sparkly quality. The sky overhead was cloudless. It was going to be a beautiful day.

Ursula's fake death and Mercedes' real one had to be linked. I would start in one place — the last place Ursula had been seen alive. I headed for the beach.

I followed the path toward the north dunes, rather than going back toward the dining hall. It would meet up with the main boardwalk.

I started toward the beach. Ursula had been last seen at the water's edge. She would never go back there, but still the ocean seemed to hold her secrets. Buster had asked me what my theory of the crime was. I had to think it out.

Mercedes had known Ursula wasn't dead. Paul could have killed Mercedes because he thought she'd led his wife to her watery death. If he'd come back and confronted Mercedes, chances are she'd have pulled her gun out again. This time he'd overpowered her and shot her. And Mercedes had kept Ursula's secret.

But what about the Rose Box? It was

gone. Why would he take it? Was he the intended buyer? I hadn't found the connection between Paul and the Rose Box, but I would. And where was the German Cross Box?

The sun was coming up over the mountains behind me, casting an eerie glow over the windows of the chapel.

There was a couple near the door. I ducked behind a tree, not wanting to be seen. Who was going in there so early in the morning? The chapel was where the sewing kits had been displayed.

They disappeared. I covered the distance quickly. I tried the door, expecting it to be locked. Instead, it swung open. I opened it just enough to get my body through.

I moved into the shadows, waiting for my eyes to adjust to the darkness.

The space looked much bigger today, empty of people. From this side, I could see across the room, the wooden chairs in auditorium style rows facing the front. Above me, the elegant rafters soared. Several sconces were lit, casting a dim glow, and the room remained murky, bathed in the morning's early glow.

The room had a musty odor. This close to the ocean, mold must be a constant battle.

I saw movement in the anteroom along

the northern side. The sewing boxes had been in there. The tables were still up, although the display was gone. I moved next to the farthest table. We'd been standing right about here, looking at the Rose Box, when Harriet had discovered the German Cross. Two tables were between them, so the boxes had been at least twelve feet apart. Mercedes took the most valuable and the most controversial.

I heard voices outside and my heart stopped. Would someone else come in and find us in here? I caught my breath and listened. The voices grew louder, more contentious and then faded. At least two people had walked by on early morning excursions.

They were gone. I breathed out.

The couple I'd seen outside appeared on the other side of a wooden column. They were talking quietly and I couldn't hear. It looked like a man and a woman, although the man was slight. I'd be really embarrassed if this meeting was of a private nature. Buster and I had had encounters in some strange places.

The woman moved into the light from the window.

Harriet.

No, the hair was not frizzy enough. In this

early morning fog, Harriet's hair would be a bundle of wiry split ends.

I moved closer, finding the light switch halfway down on the short back wall. I turned on the lights.

They flickered at first, then bright light shone in the space. The two people in the alcove were clearly illuminated. My breath caught.

Lucy. And her Asilomar friend, Carlos — the fellow who checked our meal tickets.

"Dewey," she said, startled.

"What are you doing?"

I saw the box lid in her hand. It was filled with the stylized swastikas that Harriet had found so offensive. Lucy had taken the German Cross box. Not Mercedes.

Carlos looked sheepish. He rattled his large circle of keys.

Lucy said quietly, "I didn't mean to cause all this trouble. I just couldn't stand Harriet being so upset. I thought I could just move the thing out of the display so she wouldn't have to look at it."

"So you hid it?"

She nodded, her eyes going to the fireplace and the wood box that held kindling. I swung open the lid. The German Cross sewing kit was lying on its side, seemingly unharmed.

I sighed. Had Mercedes been killed because of a hidden box?

Lucy explained herself. "I was going to return it to Nan. It's just so offensive, I can hardly bear to touch it," she said, shuddering. She pulled forward her rolling sewing machine bag. I was sort of surprised she wasn't wearing gloves.

"That's true," Carlos said. "I unlocked the door so she could return it to its rightful owner."

"Was Mercedes in here when you hid it?"

Lucy turned her head and reached in without looking. "She was here. When Nan left, I lingered. Mercedes was locking up. I wasn't thinking clearly, I just grabbed it and put the box out of sight."

She lifted the box carefully. Carlos held open her wheeled bag.

I left her to her task. She'd have to explain to Nan what she'd done. I wouldn't want to be in her shoes. It was hard to believe an inanimate object could cause so much pain.

I hurried outside, feeling better once I hit the fresh air. I blinked and rubbed my arms, which had gotten gooseflesh in the dank chapel. Mercedes took the rose box. How surprised she must have been when she and Nan discovered two of the boxes were missing.

I'd barely gotten onto the path when I was forced to a stop. A white wooden sawhorse with orange stripes and ASB stamped on it blocked my way. Two hazard cones sat on either side. A knot of rangers stood a few feet beyond, near the deck of the pool. Two golf carts were parked haphazardly and a crew of maintenance workers stood next to them. The whole group was looking at something at their feet.

They broke apart. I saw Tony and waved him over.

"What's going on?" I asked.

"A mountain lion killed a deer right on the pool deck."

"Last night?" I asked.

"Yeah. Did you hear anything?"

I shook my head. "Should I be worried?"

"Well, we're trying to decide what needs to be done. We disagree," he said, nodding his head at his colleagues.

I could tell by the frown on his face that his point of view was not being valued in their discussion.

"What do you want to do?" I asked.

"I want the lion contained. This is too close for comfort. These people believe that only a sick or injured animal would harm a human. That's not been my experience," he said with a scowl.

"Contained?" Did that mean killed? I hoped not.

"Pellicano!"

We both looked up at the sound of our name. "I guess that means you," I said.

"Yes," he said tersely. He gave me a peck on the cheek. "You'll have to go back and go around the other way if you're heading to the beach," he said.

I went back the way he was pointing. Coming up on the chapel, I could see Lucy trudging uphill, pulling her bag. Carlos was locking the door. That kit couldn't have weighed more than ten pounds, but she looked as though she was carrying the weight of the world. I felt sorry for her.

My head was clearing, and the murkiness of the morning was being replaced by the sunshine.

On the side of the road, it was the usual scene of rough cars and bed-head surfers. I looked south to see if I could spot Paul. He wasn't at the sand bar, the place where Ursula's body was supposed to wash up. That is, if she wasn't still alive.

I wasn't going to tell him I'd seen his wife last night. Not because I owed her anything. Not after the bump on the head. But because I couldn't put her further at risk. What if Paul had killed Mercedes to get to

Ursula? What if she had given her life protecting Ursula's secret?

I walked down the beach, back to the spot where I thought Ursula had gone in.

I could see now how she'd done it. The rocks curved sharply here, the far side of them out of sight. I had been looking for her straight ahead, in the water. All she had to do was stay out of sight for a few minutes, then walk out of the water. And out of her life.

I followed her steps and saw where she'd gotten in her car. An old pickup with a camper top covered with Day-Glo peace signs was parked where her VW bus had been parked. Tune in, turn on, drop out was scrawled on the side next to a Keep Tahoe Blue bumper sticker. A woman with long braids was seated in a lawn chair nursing a rather large toddler, whose feet beat a regular rhythm on the aluminum frame. She smiled at me. Her wares for sale, earrings and beaded bracelets, were spread on a blanket in front of her.

Having made eye contact, I felt trapped into looking at her stuff. She was just trying to make a living for herself and her son, based on the tiny little penis the tot presented to me when he rolled off his mother's nipple to stare up at me.

"How are you this fine morning?" she asked me, her voice dreamy. I didn't know if it was the earliness of the hour or a chronic condition that kept her eyes half-lidded.

I wished I'd kept moving. I had no interest in hippie jewelry. "Not great. Trying to process a few things." Maybe she'd leave me alone.

"I feel your aura, and you are very stressed. Do you want me to do your cards?" she asked. A deck of Tarot sat nearby.

"No need, thanks." I tried to move away, but the little boy, now squatting in the sandy dirt, had untied my shoelace.

I bent down to retie it and searched for something to buy to get me out of this.

Next to her chair, on the tail end of the truck, were several waxy yellowish lumps. A hand-lettered sign proclaimed her hand-made soap was a cure-all. I picked up one of the misshapen pieces. It was marked $5. It would be worth five dollars to get out of here.

I grabbed one. "I'll take this."

I pulled a five from my jacket. She handed me the soap, taking her time to wrap it carefully in rice paper and tie it artfully with twine. I forced myself to wait as she pretti-fied the package. When she was done twisting the twine into the best possible bow, I grabbed it and turned, nearly tripping over the poor baby.

She called after me, "I made that from the cyaniphyta plant I found in the bog at Asilomar. Cured my pregnancy mask. Completely."

That gave me an idea. I put the soap in my pocket and headed back toward Asilomar.

Around a bend, I came face to face with Paul Wiggins. I gasped. I didn't want to see him. I knew his wife hadn't thrown herself in the ocean, but she was dead to him. I wasn't going to give her away.

I stepped back and turned to walk away. He scared me. I moved quickly, crossing the street. He followed me. I didn't look at him.

"Listen to me," he said, shouting. "I didn't kill Mercedes."

I kept walking, eyes down. Soon his shoes came into view as he caught up with me, matching my pace.

He spoke quickly. "I bet the same person that killed Ursula killed Mercedes. Those two were thick as thieves. You didn't believe Mercedes, did you when she said Ursula wasn't here? I know she was here. I put her on the plane. I wrote the check for the conference."

"Paul, step away from me, please." His presence was threatening. "Or I will call the rangers." I knew the rangers were busy. He didn't.

"Check it out, Dewey. Ursula was killed and not by me. Someone was hounding her. Things were different around our house. I haven't hit my wife in three years."

Oh yeah, right. Like I'd believe that one.

"Were you the reason I was pulled in for questioning in Mercedes' death?" Paul asked, abruptly.

That was news to me. "Are they questioning you?"

"I've been in the office for the past ten hours," he said, his face reddening even more. He scrubbed at his hair. I could see the bags under his eyes and wondered when he had last slept.

"Ten hours," he whined, when I didn't react. "And the result is the same. My wife is still missing."

"Did the police ask you what you thought happened to her?"

"I told those bastards. Someone was after her. And someone got to her."

This was a guy who knew every move his wife made. He kept track of her comings and goings. He kept track of her phone calls.

I kept quiet, moving back toward the gate. The feeling of being next to this man was creeping me out.

He kept talking, his anger with the local police the only thing on his mind. "The police aren't interested in Ursula. I gave them all of her e-mails for the last two months. She'd been corresponding with a new contact."

The casualness of his admitting to having a file on his wife was chilling. I rubbed my upper arms to release the goose bumps that had popped up there.

"Do you remember the name of the person?"

He looked off in the distance, as if trying to remember. "It was not a person's name. More like one of those silly handles that people come up with to disguise themselves."

I wondered what aliases Paul had used to track his wife. He was probably the king of covering his tracks so his wife wouldn't know what he was doing.

I felt a pang of sympathy for Ursula. She never really stood a chance. Getting together with a guy like Paul meant her fate was sealed a long time ago. He'd probably graduated from opening her mail, and checking the mileage on her car, to downloading her e-mails and tracking her movements with a GPS. She had no chance at a private life, at an independent life, at a life wholly her own.

I tucked away my sadness. I needed Paul to help me find out what happened to her.

"I remember it as something to do with quilting."

Great. That narrowed the field to twenty million or so.

Her e-mails might help me find her. "Can I see them?"

He looked at me suspiciously. "I guess. I'll get them to you later."

I hurried through the gate, hunching my shoulders, hoping Paul wouldn't follow me. There was no Mercedes to make sure he stayed away.

After the first bend in the boardwalk, I looked back. I couldn't see him. I quickened my step, breaking into a jog.

EIGHTEEN

I flashed my meal ticket and disappeared into the dining hall. Sanctuary.

Kym was standing just inside, her usually pretty face creased with worry. The rash seemed to be spreading down her neck. She caught me looking and tightened her head scarf.

"Hey, Kym." I looked past her and saw Paul pacing in front of the dining hall. I was beginning to understand Ursula's predicament a little more. Was he stalking me now?

"I'm looking for someone named Renate," Kym said. "She ordered a kosher breakfast, but hasn't claimed it. Do you know her?" She rubbed at a boil.

I had the miracle soap in my pocket. Maybe it would help. Anything was better than watching Kym tearing up her skin with her long fingernails.

I offered it to her. A peace offering — better late than never.

Her eyebrow shot up. "What's this?" she said suspiciously. She lifted the package to her nose and sniffed. She shot me a withering look as though I'd laid a turd in her hand.

"It's an herbal soap," I said. "So it doesn't smell great. The flower it came from is supposed to have healing properties."

"Why do you care if I itch or not?" she said, rubbing the inside of her wrist on the table edge.

Good question. I decided not to answer it. I was fast losing my appetite watching Kym scratch. I grabbed a coffee and yogurt to go.

Carlos was in position at the kitchen window. He owed me.

"Can you get me out through the kitchen?" I said. "There's someone out front who's bugging me."

He nodded and quietly led me through the kitchen. The door came out just down the hill from Merrill Hall, out of sight of the front where Paul was pacing. I hurried away, heading back to my room to fetch my laptop.

I had a theory that needed testing. Paul had told me that they lived in Lowell, Massachusetts. That was home to the New

England Quilt Museum. I wondered if the museum fit in. Nan had mentioned buying kits from museums. Was that Ursula's connection?

I sat down in the living room and called Vangie from my keyboard. Thankfully, she was at work early and answered my ping.

Her face appeared, her pigtails pixilated. "The store has burned to a crisp, the bank accounts have been emptied, and yes, we miss you very much," she said.

"You have a funny way of telling me everything's okay," I said.

"You overestimate your presence here. We are doing fine without you," she pouted.

"I'm not calling to check up on you. I need you to make a call for me. Call the head of acquisitions at the Lowell Quilt Museum."

"Why?" Vangie asked.

"Because I need information." I filled her in on the missing sewing box.

"Oh boy, we're playing detective?" she said. "Who am I?"

"You're a young woman who knows nothing about quilting."

"So far, so good," Vangie cracked.

I spun a tale. "You've inherited your mother's house and in the attic was an old trunk. It was full of fabrics, laces, and sewing tools. It hadn't been opened for years."

"Achoo. Don't forget I'm allergic to dust."

"More like allergic to dusting," I said. Vangie laughed. "The stuff is in mint condition. Ask for a list of appraisers."

"Got it," Vangie said.

"No wait. Ask them if they accept donations. I particularly want to know about the sewing tools."

"What's going on there, Dewey?"

"It's complicated. But here's some news. Kym's here."

"Get out of town!" Vangie cried. "What do you mean, she's there?"

"She's in charge of Sewing-by-the-Sea. She'd been working for the original director, who died."

"Died? When were you going to tell me about that?"

"I told you. It's complicated."

Vangie was more interested in my family dynamics anyhow. She knew that Kym and I were like oil and water. She'd barely tolerated Kym when she'd worked at QP and was happy to see her fired. "So you and Kym, huh? I'm sorry I'm not there to see that. Is she talking to you?"

"Barely."

"Is your brother there? Where's Kevin?"

"AWOL. I don't have a clue, and Kym's

not telling."

"This is juicy stuff. Is that her new job now, running conferences?" Vangie said.

"I don't really know. How's business for real?"

Vangie gave me the condensed version of the last couple of days. Sales were okay, classes were running about two-thirds full.

"Awesome. I'm going to want to contact Cinnamon Ramstad, the teacher I've got now. She's great and I'd like her to teach for us."

Vangie said, "Noted. Look at the widget I've put on the site. It's a virtual design board. The customer drags fabric on it to plan her quilt."

"I'll check it out later. For now, please make that call, and if you get a list of appraisers, fax it to the Asilomar office and I'll pick it up after my class."

I was seated at the table in the classroom by nine o'clock. This was our fourth day of class. Some people were late, and the teacher seemed to sense our lagging energy. Lucy snuck in just as Cinnamon was beginning. She must have returned the German Cross box to Nan. She looked sad. The death of Mercedes was dragging everyone down.

Cinnamon was determined to lift our

mood. "All right everyone," she said, clapping her hands. "Give me your cameras."

We complied and she said, "I'm going to download your shots on my computer and we'll all look at them."

Cinnamon put the images from our cameras onto her screen and projected them on the wall. A continuous slide show of images flickered by. She dimmed the lights somewhat, without making the place completely dark.

She called on each person to explain their pictures. Each image was up for several seconds and then gone. There were many shots of the ocean. The obligatory gulls wheeling. Ravens in mid-squawk. Deer feeding. Frothy waves and swirling sands.

I was the only one who chose to go inside the buildings with my camera. My images of fireplaces, wood beams, and closeups of images flickered by.

"Bold choice, Dewey," Cinnamon said, making me swell with pride. "Can you explain?"

"For me, the architecture is just as important as the seascape," I said, feeling a little silly. Putting my feelings about architecture into words felt inadequate. "The buildings were designed to complement the natural setting. I like that intersection."

"Art is juxtaposition," Cinnamon said. "I'll be interested to see where you go with this."

I felt panicky. Me, too. I had no faith that I could make something interesting from the shots I had taken.

Cinnamon turned the lights on.

"Are you inspired? I hope so. Now get out your background pieces and finish piecing. Let the ideas percolate as you sew."

I was behind, having missed most of the class yesterday afternoon. Many of the students had finished work on their background pieces. Lucy pinned her piece on the wall behind us.

"Wow," I said. "You got a lot done."

"I've been here late every night, and early every morning, except for today."

"It shows. Good for you." I vowed to spend the evening here.

I'd gotten my center piece cut out and pinned that up. I cut out triangles and laid them around the middle. I tried to imagine what images to put in the large space. I was using ocean colors for the backgrounds, blue-grays, greens, and the watery light blue that the sea took on in the late afternoon sun.

I looked at a picture I'd taken of the trusses in Merrill Hall. Repeated over and over, the pointed shape became a prayer of symmetry and structure. The trusses were essential, holding up the roof of the building, but the beauty of the wood and the symmetry of the repeated design transcended mere function.

I couldn't imagine how to incorporate that into my quilt.

I set up my sewing machine, threading it with blue-gray thread that would blend with the fabrics I'd chosen. I'd heard about the meditative quality of sewing the same block over and over. Ina had told me her best thinking was done at the machine.

I played with fabrics, cutting small pieces and placing them on the piece of flannel I'd brought along as a design wall. I stood back to get the effect.

"You can use your camera, Dewey," Lucy said. "Try looking through the viewfinder. It makes everything small and smushed together. You'll catch right away any colors that are wrong."

Cinnamon approached and moved away a bright green print. The combination immediately looked more appetizing.

"How'd you do that?" I asked, in awe of her ability to know what was needed.

"Years of practice."

"I was afraid you were going to say that. I

don't have years. I've got customers who rely on me to help them put together great quilts."

Cinnamon smiled, tossing her long braid. She leaned in, whispering conspiratorially, "Here's one secret. Black. Everything looks a little better on black. Also, remember you want a variety of scales. You want large prints, small prints. What I used to do was find one fabric, with a lot of colors that I really liked and use that as my jumping-off point."

"Some of it's just intuitive, isn't it?" I was sure I'd been born without the good color gene.

"I don't believe that," Cinnamon said. "I can teach you to have a good eye."

She smiled and continued around the room, admiring a fabric choice, exclaiming over a photo.

She talked as we worked. "Let your mind wander. I'll be printing out pictures from your camera for you to look at, but don't hold them too tight in your mind. We're not going for a literal interpretation here. Ideas will swirl in your mind, if you let them. Sift through them gently. Don't reject anything, but don't accept the first thought you have, either. There's more meat in the marrow. Get to the marrow."

I fed triangles under my presser foot, making sure to keep the edges aligned and using the quarter-inch foot to get my seam right. After the first couple, I found the rhythm and felt my mind wander.

The pictures that I'd taken were playing up on the wall. I'd taken pictures of the Pirates' Den specifically to show Lucy. I watched as my photos cycled through.

"Hey Lucy," I said. "Do you know what room your grandfather lived in?"

She looked up and stopped her sewing while the den flickered by. "He doesn't mention a specific room. Seemed like they were housed in barracks. Besides, I think the building had been reconfigured in the fifties when the state took over Asilomar.

"Nice shot," Lucy said, after watching my pictures slide by. She was teasing.

I looked up to see I'd taken a picture of the floor plan that showed the emergency exits. What a geek. I laughed, glad to have a moment of levity with her.

I didn't stop until the bell sounded the start of lunch.

Cinnamon dismissed us. "Go eat. After lunch, we'll get out your blueprints and rinse them."

My blueprint fabric? Where was it? I reached into my bag for the plastic bag she'd given us. It wasn't there. Shoot. I bopped my hand on my forehead. Dumb mistake. My fingers brushed against the welt Ursula had given me and I saw stars.

Harriet saw my discomfort. "What's wrong?" she asked.

"I've lost my fabric," I confessed. The twinkles, and the pain, faded. I had to remember not to make any sudden moves. "I can't remember what I did with it."

We streamed out of the building. Cinnamon locked the door behind us, pulling it shut with a jerk. Lucy and Harriet and I started toward the dining hall.

"When did you last have it?" Harriet said. "Retrace your steps. Let your mind wander," she said, imitating Cinnamon's languid delivery.

I laughed, but it worked. I remembered, I'd been headed to the Pirates' Den to retrieve it when I met Ursula.

I broke off when we crossed the road.

"I have to make a detour," I said, without going into detail. "I'll join you guys at lunch."

I hustled across the street and over to the building that housed Mercedes' office. Yellow crime scene tape stretched across the door of the room on the lower level where she'd died but there was no evidence of police. They must have finished processing the scene.

Coming up the steps to the den's living room, I heard sobbing. Loud and uncensored, it sounded like a toddler weeping at the mall, having been kept out past bedtime. I stopped dead, wondering if I should intrude.

I looked in the doorway. Kym was standing in front of a mirror, wailing, her thin shoulders shaking with effort. I came behind her so I could see her reflection. She'd taken off her scarf and was leaning in, studying her face.

This was the same mirror I'd caught sight of Ursula in.

"Kym?"

She moaned when she saw me. Her fingers twisted in the scarf as though she was trying to keep them from scratching. Her cheeks were riven with tears.

Her features twisted. A sob escaped and she used her hands to stop herself. Her misery was not alleviated by the sight of me.

I waded in anyhow. This was my brother's wife. I couldn't walk out, pretending I hadn't seen her. I stood next to her. "Are you okay?"

That dumb question earned me a withering glance. My sister-in-law was nothing if not consistent in her disdain of me.

"I thought everyone was at lunch," she said. "I just needed a moment alone."

She sniffed loudly, using her hand to wipe away her tears. She flinched as she brushed one of the open boils.

"Your face looks better," I lied.

She rubbed the skin under her neck. The tiniest of wattles was growing there.

"It's worse. Whatever was in that soap, it made it worse."

Oops.

"I'm not crying about my face," she said, but I didn't believe her.

She continued, "It's this flipping conference. People are complaining left and right. I can't get a moment's peace. They walk in here all morning long, just one fucking whiner after another."

Kym didn't use words like that. I felt a giggle escape, and caught it with the back of my hand. Like most difficult people, Kym couldn't cope when confronted with other's needs.

Kym wound her scarf around her head, checking herself one last time in the mirror. She walked over to the desk and sat down. I glanced around the room for my blueprint fabric. I hoped the cleaning crew hadn't thrown it out. I checked the trash can just in case.

Nothing. Damn.

Kym slammed down a folder. The back of her hands looked puffy.

"My room's too coooold," she said in a dead-on imitation of Concordia's reedy voice. She continued, imitating her tormentors. "Too dark. The projector's not working, the floor's too slippery."

She continued, "One woman was in here earlier complaining that there was a deer outside her window." She looked at me plaintively. "What am I supposed to do about that?"

She was pathetic. I said, "What would Mercedes do?"

A vision of a rubber bracelet with WWMD? on it flitted across my mind, and I stifled another giggle. Kym's discomfort notwithstanding, seeing her trying to make order out of chaos felt like payback for all the trouble she'd caused me.

"I don't think Mercedes had this kind of upset. Everyone was holding on to their complaints for me."

I doubted that. I'd seen Mercedes in action. She could handle the tough cookies and make them feel like they were having the time of their lives.

Kym was still going on. "The dining hall keeps screwing up the special meals. I've got someone in a sugar coma. Or so she says. She looks perfectly fine to me."

I almost felt sorry for her. She was so far in over her head. She didn't have the diplomatic or dictatorial skills that Mercedes had, necessary to rule three hundred middle-aged women.

I came up short at the sight of Kym opening the lid of a laptop.

NINETEEN

That got my attention. Kym and computers had not been on speaking terms the last I knew.

"Yours?" I asked. Mercedes' laptop had been in her room and confiscated as part of the police investigation. I'd given up hope at getting to her files. Now I saw a glimmer of opportunity.

She nodded. "Mercedes insisted I get one."

That was interesting. "Is it a clone of hers?" I asked.

Kym frowned, not understanding. I clarified. "Is it the same as hers — with the same files?"

Kym shrugged.

I heard the familiar noises of the operating system booting. "Do you actually know how to use it?"

Kym and computers were like oil and water. Like Peets and Starbucks. Like Paris and Nicole.

"No."

"What are you trying to do?" I said, itching to take it away from her. with access to the registration files, I could find out where Ursula had been, and maybe where she was hiding now.

Kym said, "There's another Sewing-by-the-Sea session due to start in a little over eight weeks. All the teachers and customers need to know that Mercedes has died, but I have no idea how to do that. If I can find their addresses, I'll write to each of them."

She indicated a pile of envelopes and a large roll of stamps. She had a box of writing paper with a picture of kittens and yarn watermarked on the pink sheets. The envelopes matched, of course.

"How many?" I said.

"Same as this one. Three hundred, more or less, including teachers."

"Don't you have e-mail?" I asked.

Kym looked at me blankly.

I went on. "Mercedes e-mailed me, so she must have addresses for everyone."

She shrugged. "Mercedes has some kind of database thingy, but I need Kevin's help for that. For now, I'm just going to handwrite all of them."

"Yikes, Kym. Are you kidding me? You

could send out one blast e-mail and let everyone know in five minutes. Your way will take hours."

Her lower lip trembled. She was five seconds away from a major technological meltdown. How my sister-in-law had lived her twenty-six years in Silicon Valley without learning how to use a computer amazed me. She acted as if she was Amish and the computer was verboten. She relied on Kevin for everything.

"Give me the computer," I said. Kym pushed it in my direction, but not all the way, making me reach to pull it the last couple of inches.

I was excited when I looked at the screen. Mercedes' anal nature spilled into her computer files. She'd copied everything on to Kym's laptop. There were folders lined up on the desktop, each one neatly labeled. Each Sewing-by-the-Sea had its own folder. One for each of the latest sessions, and two more in the future, July and October.

I opened the one marked July 2009. An excel spreadsheet held all the attendees' information: name, home address, phone numbers, method of payment. And e-mail addresses. The list was long, over three hundred lines. I didn't want to have to send a message to each one.

I opened Kym's e-mail program. From the look of the unopened messages, I was the first one to open this program. It was a Sewing-by-the-Sea account. A half-dozen unopened messages from Mercedes were in the inbox.

It didn't need a password. There was no way Kym could remember one.

Yes. Mercedes had forwarded to Kym the welcome message she'd sent to all the July seminar participants ten days ago. When I opened it and hit reply, all of the names were already in the header. All I had to do was create a new file and send it to out to this group. It would take minutes.

I looked at Kym, who was rubbing her arms, her legs squeezed tightly together. Her hives seemed to still be spreading. I caught myself scratching my neck. I really hoped my soap hadn't made things worse. That hadn't been my intention.

Kym didn't have to know how easy this w . For one thing, she wouldn't appreciate what I'd done unless I made it look a little hard. I'd tell her this was going to take some time and effort and spend my time looking for a trace of Ursula Wiggins.

"I'm going to be a while," I said to Kym.

"Hurry up," she said, ever gracious.

"Why don't you write down what you

want to say?" I suggested.

I knew she was just being knee-jerk upset with me. She had no understanding of computers whatsoever. I was free to take my time in the files.

I'd see what trace of Ursula I could detect. If her usual room was listed, I might find her today. My heart beat faster at the idea.

I opened the file marked May 2009. I found my name and personal info. I did a search for Ursula's name that came up empty. Mercedes had been telling the truth. She wasn't scheduled for this year. But Paul had said he'd written a check.

I looked for an accounting program to see if Mercedes had deposited his money, but couldn't find one. Her books weren't on here. She didn't trust Kym with her finances.

I went back to the roster files. Each year had four seminars named by the month they were held. Chances were Ursula came to the May session each year, so I decided to start there. I began with the 2008 file and went backward. Ursula's name didn't appear until 2003. Paul had said she'd been coming for ten years. I went back to 1999. She was listed there and for the next four years. She fell off the roster in 2003.

But she kept coming. Where did she stay?

I knew the way Asilomar worked. The organizer received the keys to all the rooms and doled them out to the participants. She was responsible to let Asilomar know who was in each room so they could charge accordingly. At the end of the weekend, the person in charge collected keys and returned them to Asilomar. Mercedes had said she was responsible to Asilomar. This was what she meant.

If Ursula was staying here, her name would have to show up somewhere. Ursula talked about "her" room. I'd gotten the impression she'd stayed in the same one each time. One would be unaccounted for.

Mercedes kept detailed records, matching each participant with their dorm room and their roommates. I looked through the assignments. These women were creatures of habit, returning to the same space year after year.

I went back to 2003. There she was. No roommate. Paul had paid extra for Ursula to have a single. Of course, so no one would see her bruises.

Mercedes put her in the same place. For the four years between 1999 and 2003, she'd stayed in Room 1626. I looked on the roster for 2004. That room was listed as Mercedes'. But Mercedes stayed in 505 every year. The room she'd died in.

Bingo! Ursula had to be in there. I didn't know what building Room 1626 was in, but I should be able to find out at the front desk. I wrote the number down and stuffed the note in my pocket.

"Here's my letter," Kym said, shoving a scrap piece of yellow-lined paper under my nose. I minimized the accommodations file and took the letter. It was short and to the point.

"Okay, great. Just give me a minute to type it up."

I composed the e-mail and sent it out quickly. I closed the laptop, waiting for her thank you. She was frowning.

"You didn't show me what you did."

"You wrote it. I just copied it and e-mailed it."

Her lower lip trembled. My head began to throb. I rubbed my hairline where Ursula had hit me, feeling my fingers soothe the spot.

"What?" I said.

"It's so . . . impersonal," she said. Her lips were pursed. She twisted the ends of her scarf making it tighten around her face un-attractively.

The girl was never satisfied. I hadn't worked with her for six months, and five minutes into this, I'd had enough. Even with this simple task, she was impossible to please.

"I'm taking a class here, Kym and I've got to go back to it." I'd spent most of my lunch hour here. If I rushed over to the Administration building, I could get a sandwich from the store cooler, find out what room Ursula was staying in, and still get to my class on time to show off my key print.

The blueprint fabric. Damn I hadn't found that. I stood up, looking around the room.

"Kym, did you see a piece of blueprint fabric in here? I was getting ready to expose it . . ."

Kym said, "You never should have come to this conference. You're the one causing all the problems here. I *told* her not to cash your check."

"Excuse me?" I stopped in mid-scan. I saw the plastic bag on the table under the window.

Kym crossed her arms, then uncrossed and scratched. "The minute I saw your name on the form, I told Mercedes you'd be nothing but trouble. If it had been up to me, I would have lost your registration."

My mouth fell open. Kym was looking at me with complete disdain.

No wonder Mercedes hated me from the get go. My darling sister-in-law had been filling her head about me. Nothing nice, by the sounds of it. I never stood a chance with Mercedes. Kym had gotten there first.

"Face it, Dewey, you're no quilter. And you never will be."

Whatever pity I'd been feeling for her vanished. I was left with a familiar feeling — disgust that I'd let myself get taken in again by Kym.

I grabbed my fabric and let myself out without saying another word.

I was back to my classroom before I realized I'd meant to stop at the registration desk to find out about Ursula. The Legendary Quilts students were gathered outside. I couldn't leave without drawing a lot of attention to myself.

Cinnamon had a table set up outside the door with a half-dozen buckets of water on it. I joined the group.

Lucy said, "We're exposing our images to the sunlight."

"That's how the magic happens," Cinnamon said. "Come on, everyone, let's see what you've got."

"Just dip your piece in the water. Swish it around gently."

The first group of six stepped up and

rinsed their pieces. They spread them on the bushes nearby. We gathered around, looking at the pieces of blueprint fabric. Ghostly images were appearing. A fish skeleton, a spray of oleander, seaweed.

"What's that?" one of the students cried, pointing to a squiggly line next to a sand dollar.

Cinnamon looked over her shoulder. "You got an image of a thread. You've got to make sure no random things hit the cloth. Everything will be imprinted."

Cinnamon directed me. "Rinse it in the water."

I dunked mine. The water turned lime and the fabric changed, going through the spectrum of color between green and blue. It was the color of the ocean near the shore.

I laid the fabric out on a bench. The outline of the key appeared slowly, then the details emerged. The image got more distinct. I grinned up at Lucy.

"Cool," I said.

"The sharpness will be determined by the amount of sunshine your piece got," Cinnamon said, circling behind us and watching.

Lucy showed me her piece. Squiggly lines appeared. "It's a piece of bark."

I glanced at my piece again. To my chagrin, another image was emerging on the edge of the fabric.

"Oh, no," I said. "I ruined it."

"How?" Cinnamon asked. She bent down and looked at the fabric.

I shook my head. "I confess, I lost track of my fabric after I put the key on it. It was lying in the living room all night. Who knows what was laid on top of it."

"Not ruined, just different than you'd intended," Cinnamon said. "No mistakes, just a design opportunity."

It didn't feel like an opportunity. It felt like a screw-up.

I watched the image appear. It looked familiar. First, the distinct ninety-degree angle that the clamp took. The wings came next.

Then the body.

This was a sewing bird. The missing sewing bird.

I searched my backpack for the Polaroid Mercedes had taken of the Rose Box. That was where I'd seen that particular shape. The sewing bird that would make the Rose Box worth a small fortune. It matched.

I followed everyone back into the classroom, quietly mulling over what this meant.

The sewing bird had been in the Pirates' Den, sometime between the time I'd left and presumably Mercedes' murder. The person who had both the Rose Box and the sewing bird could sell it. For a lot of money.

The killer had the box. Who had the sewing bird? If the killer had both, she was scot free. And rich.

I worked on my quilt for the rest of the afternoon, my mind on what I'd learned.

Ursula was alive. She'd been in the Pirates' Den. She had been here, right under our noses, the entire time. I didn't think she'd killed Mercedes. She'd been too startled when she learned about her death. As soon as I found her and talked to her myself, I'd tell Tony where she was.

Class was over at four, and we all left. Cinnamon gave us our question to ponder overnight: What place does quilting have in your life?

The first day Cinnamon had asked us what we were running away from. After my experience with Kym earlier, I knew I'd been running from her. And with good reason. The two of us would never see eye to eye on what was important in life. She'd risked her health for a beauty treatment, she refused to learn how to use the computer, and she felt my brother was her personal errand boy.

I wanted my relationship with Buster to

be on equal footing. We met as equals and I wanted it to stay that way. Kevin and Kym were like a couple from my parents' era. He brought home the bacon and she fried it. She kept herself pretty and youthful looking, and he pretended to rule the roost. Her playing at this job for Mercedes just showed how immature she was. She was unable to handle the smallest glitch. I couldn't imagine her taking over for Mercedes.

I'd taken action when I'd fired her last year, but I'd never really lived up to the consequences of my action. The shop had suffered. We lost customers and, if I was brutally honest, some of my mother's reputation. We'd been seen as a family business, but now there was a rift in the family, and that made some people uncomfortable. I needed to repair it without losing my integrity as the shop owner.

Taking this class had been a form of running away, too. Vangie had nailed it when she'd said it was an indulgence, but that wasn't completely right. I needed this class for myself. Needed to know that I could grow as a quilter. My eyes had opened thanks to this class, not just to nature and the images we view as iconic. Cinnamon asked us to go beneath, go deeper into what we saw.

With Ursula, at first, I'd seen a woman who was pathetic. Someone who took her own life rather than live. The ultimate running away. But she turned out to be running toward something. A new life. Ursula, under the worst conditions for a woman, had been determined to carve out a life worth living. She'd managed to escape her husband's net and start over.

I wasn't sure yet how she'd done it. It was obvious that she'd needed money. She looked to Mercedes for help, and Mercedes, knowing her situation, had given her a way out.

I headed for the Administration building. As I walked past the sleeping rooms, I looked for the number I'd written down. There were a lot of rooms at Asilomar, spread over several acres. I had a feeling Ursula was in one of the ones far out of the way.

TWENTY

I went to the desk. "I'm looking for my friend. She's in room 1626. Can you direct me there?"

"Certainly."

The man in the polyester blue vest pulled out a manila-colored map. He turned the map to face me and circled a building I hadn't seen before. It sat on the northern-most point of Asilomar, facing the dunes.

He said, "If you walk out here, past the chapel and the lodge, and go up the hill, you'll see Viewpoint. She's in that build-ing."

"Thank you."

I started to walk away and remembered the assignment I'd given Vangie. I turned back. "Did you get a fax for me? Dewey Pel-licano?"

The young man smiled. He went into a small private office and came back with two sheets of paper.

Faxes from the QP office. Vangie had outdone herself. Not only had she gotten a list of appraisers from the Lowell Quilt Museum, she'd called the San Jose Museum of Quilts and Textiles and got their recommendations as well.

I sat outside on the Adirondack chair and looked them over.

The lists were different. There were plenty of experts on the east coast and more here on the west coast. I didn't see any overlap. I looked at the Lowell fax. There were several familiar names. Nan Orchard. Quentin Rousseau.

I shuffled pages and perused the pages from the local museum. One name jumped out at me. Mercedes Madsen.

Mercedes was a certified appraiser, so she would have known exactly what the Rose Box was worth and what was needed to make it valuable. An appraiser would know who was in the market for antique sewing tools.

It stood to reason that if Mercedes was using this opportunity to get her hands on the sewing box, she'd invited Nan here planning to steal the box from her. Had she found the missing tool? Or invited the person that owned the tool. Did Kym know?

My sister-in-law was the perfect foil. She

didn't know anything about antiques. She had some knowledge of quilts, but I doubted that she knew anything about sewing tools.

I folded the pages and stuck them in my backpack.

I went to room 1626 and knocked on the door. It was down at the end in the back of a building that had a great view of the sunset. This room overlooked the road, which was lined with scrub oaks and grasses.

I tried the door but nothing budged. I banged again.

Where would Ursula be? She couldn't spend time outdoors. Paul was out there. She had no place to go.

I called to her, being careful not to use her name. "It's Dewey. Can I talk to you?" I whispered.

Nothing but silence. I waited, trying to sense if the room was empty or not. I could hear nothing. No breathing.

I moved away from Ursula's door, down the concrete sidewalk that ran in front of the rest of the rooms in the building. I knocked on doors as I went. About three doors down, someone answered my knock.

"Yes?" A pretty blonde answered. She was at least fifty years old, her hair streaked with gray but perfectly coiffed.

"I'm looking for the woman in Room

1626," I said. "Do you know her?"

"Yes, that's my friend June."

"What does June look like?" I asked, my heart racing. Was I close to finding Ursula?

"She's tiny, with black hair."

My heart sunk. Definitely not Ursula.

"Are you sure?"

"Of course I am. We've been coming here every year for the past five years. We always get the same rooms. We enjoy the raccoons. They come out at night, taking the peanuts we leave for them along the railing."

I hurried away, creeped out by the idea of the raccoons so close to their sleeping rooms.

Maybe I'd copied the number down wrong.

I trudged back to my room. It was a long walk, thankfully mostly downhill. Where to look for Ursula now? I thought about how she'd appeared in the mirror in the Pirates' Den living room. Where had she come from?

I was waylaid by the sight of Buster's truck parked in the lot outside the Stuck-Ups Inn, right next to my car. My heart did a little leap.

I ran to the building, and into the living room. Buster was waiting for me in one of the deep armchairs. He smiled when he saw me, and stood up. The creases his smile dug into his face gave me a jolt of happiness. I kissed him hello, pushed him back into the chair, and sat on his lap.

"This is a surprise. What are you doing here?" I asked.

"I'm done. The case went to the jury."

"Finally," I said, settling deeper into his arms. He'd shaved, probably in the car with his electric razor. His chin was super smooth. He could get a five o'clock shadow by 1:30 most days. I appreciated his desire to look good for me, and rubbed my hand on his jaw.

"I'm off for the next four days. No work for me until Monday morning."

"Sounds good," I said. I meant it. I could feel my breathing slow. I stroked his hair. The worries of the day faded.

Buster would help me find Ursula and the missing sewing box. I could explain to him my theories and he'd help me figure things out — one of the perks of having a homicide detective for a boyfriend. I'd bounced things off him and together we'd hit on insights that I wouldn't have gotten to on my own.

"I'm all yours," he said.

I rehearsed what I was going to tell him. How I was going to lay out the facts. I made mental lists of the players.

But for now I was just going to enjoy the

security of his lap.

"Except for tonight," he said into my neck.

I sat up, wrenching my hand away from his silky locks. "What's that?"

He grimaced as I accidentally pulled out a hair.

I searched his face. His eyes were restless. He was acting like a puppy who was about to pee on the rug. Knowing he was about to do something wrong, but unable to stop himself.

"Spit it out, Healy. You can't lie to me."

"The mountain lion made a kill this morning," he said eagerly.

"I know, I saw it."

"Cool, huh? The thing is, the best time to track a lion is after she's made a kill like that." He sat forward, practically dumping me from his lap. I held onto the edge of the chair, twisting to watch his animated face.

"What's that got to do with you?" I said.

"She caches her food, half-burying it so she can come back and feed again. Tony and I are staking out the pool to see if she comes back."

"How do you know all this?" I asked.

"Tony called me this morning."

"Again?" I didn't mind when Tony had called him earlier in the week because he knew I'd needed Buster with me, but about this? I felt a little hurt.

Buster didn't notice. "He asked me to bring your dad's rifle, and he said I could come along on the hunt if I wanted to."

Amazing. Buster sounded like a ten-year-old who'd been invited to play stickball with the big kids.

Buster had always been around my house growing up. He and my brother Kevin had been best friends. Tony, at six years older than those two, had been a demigod to the younger boys. Buster and Kevin had been allowed to clean off his skateboard, wax his surfboard, and wash his car.

We'd all idolized Tony. He was the strongest, fastest kid on the block. But he'd left home at seventeen to go to college. School and then work and the mountains kept him away much of the time. The more he stayed away, the greater his status in the neighborhood. Any time he came home, he was likely to attract a gang of younger kids that dogged him. Buster had always been leader of the pack.

"The lion roams an area of up to sixty miles," he said.

Buster launched into a description of what they'd be looking for. Marks on the trees, dead deer. I stopped listening.

He was way too enthusiastic about this

job. "I didn't know you knew anything about mountain lions," I said coolly.

"I'm learning. They're fascinating."

"Is it dangerous?" I asked.

"Hey, you're sitting on a homicide detective for the San Jose PD. Tracking a mountain lion can't be more dangerous than that."

"That's not an answer."

"Would your big brother put me in danger?"

"Again, not an answer."

"Babe . . ."

I gave him the evil eye. He knew how much I hated being called Babe.

"Don't you trust Tony?"

I pouted. "I'm not so sure. He thinks he can talk to the animals or something."

"The cougar whisperer."

I moved Buster's hand out of my lap, and stood up. "It's not a joke. He's got some kind of hotline to the wildlife psyche. But what if he's wrong? What if you're not safe?"

Buster gathered me in his arms, and pulled me in for a kiss, settling for the cheek I turned on him. Now I saw the backpack on the floor. It was stuffed, with three water bottles hanging from the side. He was really doing this.

"We won't be gone long," he said into my ear.

I stroked the skin on the inside of his wrist. He was wearing his leather thong. I caught my pinkie under it and tugged.

"Are you planning to spend the night out there?"

"No, we'll just poke around the woods for a few hours."

"Look at your face," I said. "You're all excited about the prospect of spending time with Tony."

"It's a very manly thing to do."

"Camp with my brother?"

"Hunting for a mountain lion."

"Don't bring home any carcasses. Don't go caveman on me."

"Just think how virile I will be after the hunt."

"Get out of my sight."

"I'll make it up to you."

"Don't give me that," I said. "You're blowing me off to spend time with my brother."

"You're busy."

I was going to be. I was going to make the most of my time. I would track down Ursula and get her to tell me what she knew about the sewing kit.

Tony and Buster were meeting in the Administration building. I walked over with him. Buster was practically humming with excitement as he handed Tony the nylon bag that held Dad's rifle.

Tony was equally revved up. It was kind of cute. "We've got to go get in position. I convinced the others to rope off the area and to leave the deer alone, so there's a good chance the lion will come back to feed."

"Where will you be?"

"Well hidden," Tony said, pointing into the forest that surrounded Asilomar. "No one will be able to tell where we are."

I indicated the bag. "Are you going to kill it?"

Tony looked affronted. "Of course not. We want to observe, that's all."

So the rifle was for protection. I pushed down the image of a mountain lion stalking my two favorite guys. That didn't happen in real life.

I gave them both a quick kiss. "Go, hunt."

They turned, chattering.

"Wait!" I said. I ran back to where they were. "Tony, what's going on with Mercedes' murder investigation?" I asked.

"The police are handling it. They're finished with the crime scene and have released the room."

His mind was clearly on the mountain

lion. I waved him off and he and Buster disappeared, seeming to forget about me as soon as they turned their backs.

Twenty-One

My stomach growled. I'd missed most of the dinner hour, but I still had time to grab something to eat.

The room was nearly empty, with dirty plates on most of the tables. The cleanup crew was in full swing. The noise of ceramic hitting ceramic filled the space. The servers talked in a group in back by the coffee station. I went into the hall and got a dinner from the kitchen window. I'd barely made the end of service.

I passed a ranger sitting at a table. She looked up as I approached.

"Did you have a cell phone in Ms. Madsen's room?" she asked. "We're returning them to their owners."

"I did," I said, feeling a frisson of excitement that my phone was going to be back in my backpack.

"Your number?" she consulted a list in front of her. The police had inventoried the phones. I had no doubt that they'd had a list of everyone's phone calls.

I told her.

"Your ID, please," she said. I showed her my license. She checked my name off the list, pulled my cell from a tote bag parked on the chair beside her, and handed it to me.

I smiled at her. I could see I had several new messages. I was connected again. Whoopee.

I took my phone and my chicken cutlet to an empty table. I listened to Vangie telling me about the faxes, and a message from Buster saying he'd be down tonight. Pearl and Ina had called several days ago, passing the phone back and forth and exhorting me to do well at my conference.

I was nearly finished when Freddy joined me, putting his domed dish next to mine, and grabbing a breadstick.

"I'm starved," he said, taking the plastic cover off and digging in. I guessed his diet was about to be broken for good.

"Why are you so late?" I asked, clicking my phone closed and putting it in my pocket. I already felt better dressed.

He grimaced. "The neediest of all needy students. She's single-handedly taken the fun out of dysfunction. She hasn't done a lick of work all week, and today she couldn't understand why everyone else was so far ahead. With one day left of class, she was trying to do four days of work. It was all I could do not to bop her on the head so I could get over here and get some sustenance before tonight."

He sighed heavily as he took a bite of broccoli.

"Did you hear?" he said. "There's a memorial service for Mercedes."

"Really? Who put that together?" I could guarantee it wasn't my sister-in-law.

"Quentin, mostly. He's big on marking occasions. Being from New Orleans, he's probably trying to line up a funeral jazz band right now. You think there are any in Monterey County?"

"Mariachi, maybe," I said, laughing.

We ate quietly for a few minutes. As my stomach filled, my mind returned to trying to find Ursula and what it meant that she had the sewing bird. Would she go to the service? She could, incognito. Mercedes was the only one who really knew what she looked like. And Paul, of course.

What if he came?

Maybe Freddy could help. "Freddy, I saw Ursula Wiggins."

"Who? I don't know who that is."

"The woman I thought threw herself in the ocean on Tuesday."

He drew back. "And you saw her when?"

"Yesterday," I said, rubbing my head where she'd hit me. It felt better, but was still sore to the touch.

Freddy pointed a fusilli at me. His eyebrows were arched like a kabuki actor. "So she faked her own death?"

I nodded.

"Whoa," Freddy stopped chewing.

"Don't tell anyone. Her abusive husband is wandering around here and I don't want him to know she's still here. He might try to kill her or something."

"Boy, Pellicano, you sure fall in with a rough crowd."

Freddy had been at the Quilt Extravaganza last year where two women had been murdered.

"You never met her?" I said. "She used to come here."

"Unless she was one of my students, I don't think so."

"I don't think she ever took a class," I said.

Freddy scooped up the last remaining bit of sauce off his plate with his finger and smacked his lips. He leaned back and rubbed his belly.

"That hit the spot. Have you figured out

who killed Mercedes yet?"

"Me?" I said. "Why would you think that?"

Freddy looked at me askance. "Is that how you want to play it? Little Miss Innocence?"

"Mercedes was killed. The police are looking into it," I said.

"I thought I saw your darling boy-toy earlier," Freddy said. "I figured maybe you and him . . ."

"He's not around right now," I said, trying to shut down Freddy's inquiring mind.

"Do I detect trouble in paradise?" he said, his nose for trouble twitching. I wasn't going to discuss Buster's defection with him.

I stood up. "Shall we go pay our respects?"

I followed him to the beautiful structure up the hill from the dining hall. The sun was low in the sky and the warm sandstone seemed to catch the rays and hold them, turning the facades orangey.

Merrill Hall was buzzing with activity. It looked like every student had turned out to honor Mercedes. There were pictures of her, blown up to poster size, on easels spread around the perimeter of the huge room. In the one closest to me she looked pretty, smiling broadly. I realized she'd never smiled at me. Not once. Too bad; she was much prettier that way.

Quentin and Kym were in the front of the room, standing on the stage. Quentin was fussing with a projector screen. Kym was swathed in black from head to toe, looking like a beekeeper. She was letting Quentin do the work.

I walked through the crowd, wondering if Mercedes' murderer would show up. I wasn't alone in that thought. In the back corner, nearly hidden by a support post that held up the loft was the Pacific Grove detective I'd met yesterday. He was standing in the shadows, his brown suit blending into the background of the wood-paneled walls. I knew the police would do this, but he seemed so out of place, his presence was jarring. Just to me. Most of the participants didn't seem to notice him as they filed past and took their seats.

There was no sign of Ursula. She still needed to get money to get out of town. Would she try to sell the bird to someone else?

Kym might have taken the box from Mercedes' closet. If she knew that Mercedes had been hiding Ursula here, she might have put two and two together. I didn't think she had enough smarts for that, but it was possible.

I wanted to talk to Nan, to find out if she'd seen the box since it was stolen.

The group was subdued, the talk quiet and respectful. A row of votives was lighted near the picture, casting eerie shapes on the walls. Someone was playing the piano.

Of course, it was Nan. Harriet was alongside her, singing the Carole King song that Nan was playing. I was glad to see the two of them united — friends again.

But it was making it impossible for me to talk to Nan.

I waited by the piano for them to finish, fanning myself with the small program I'd been handed. Quentin had included a brief history of Mercedes' life.

Lucy joined me. "Nice work," I said, nodding at the duo. "You got them talking?" I asked.

Lucy shrugged. "Nan's promised never to display the German Cross box again until Harriet writes up an explanation. They're talking about a multi-media show with the box, some slides from Harriet's family, and a narrative about art and fear. They're going to take the box to schools and talk about their differences."

"Well, at least, some good came of it," I said. I meant it. Hiding the box away didn't solve anything. Educating made more sense.

On stage, Quentin and Kym fussed with folding chairs, setting up a few on either side of the easel. It looked like people were going to share their memories of Mercedes. I needed some fresh air.

I started down the stone steps and took a hit of ocean air. The sun was starting to set, and the sky was glowing.

I got only a few steps, when a figure stepped out from behind a tree. I screamed, but the noise was cut off by a hand over my mouth. My eyes felt like they would bug out of my head. I bit down. Hard. The hand left my face.

I wheeled around, and found Paul Wiggins, rubbing his palm. I'd gotten him right in the soft spot between his thumb and index finger.

"Jesus," he said.

"What are you doing?" I said. I was too winded to move away. I leaned on my knees and took in several deep breaths.

"Why'd you bite me?" he asked, managing to sound wounded.

"You scared the bejesus out of me. What have you been doing, following me?"

As soon as I said it, I knew that it was true. I'd felt his presence a number of times.

"Me?" He had the nerve to sound offended.

"What? You only *hit* women, you don't stalk them?" I said, angered by his nonchalance.

Paul took several steps back. "I'm going crazy, not knowing. The cops won't tell me a thing. You seem to know what's going on."

I walked away, and he kept pace. I yelled over my shoulder. "You don't want to follow me now. I'm going to meet my brother, the ranger, and my boyfriend. He's a cop in San Jose. He wouldn't want to know that you've been harassing me."

"I have the e-mails you wanted," he said.

I walked back reluctantly. I needed those e-mails. They could prove that Mercedes was after the Rose Box all along. And that Ursula was the key.

I held out my hand. "Is there evidence in there that your wife stole something?"

He pouted, clutching the pages in his fist. "You didn't want to hear it. No one wants to hear it. Everyone thinks Ursula hangs the moon — that she's the most wonderful person. Let me tell you. I'm not the only person in this relationship, you know. She's not perfect. I don't want to hit her, I really don't, but she can be the most exasperating person."

My teeth clenched. I wasn't going to listen to this creep, this bully, justify hitting his wife, but he was the only connection I had to Ursula now. I couldn't let his self-satisfied justifications get in my way. I steeled myself, smiling at him in a way that I hoped would stroke his pathetic ego.

"My wife, she has these terrible habits . . ."

He never called Ursula by name. It was always "my wife." His property to do with whatever he chose to do. My stomach grew queasy as he continued.

"What did she steal, Paul?"

He shook his head. "I don't know. She wouldn't tell me," he whined.

"Stay away from me," I said, grabbing the papers from his hand. "Next time I'll call the police."

I headed back for the memorial service, and sat in the back room, reading the e-mails. Ursula had used the screen name, LeftCoastWoman, to sign her correspondence. I recognized the recipient of several e-mails.

Nan, the sewing box lady. I found her sitting in a row with the rest of the morning crew. Sherry and Red looked up as I signaled for Nan to come out and join me. We walked to the back of the large room. There was no sign of the police detective I'd seen earlier.

"Nan, did you e-mail with Ursula Wiggins?" I asked without preamble.

She shrugged. "I don't know. I have a website, people ask me questions all the time."

"Have you met Ursula here at Sewing-by-the-Sea?"

Her fingers worried the drawstring of her linen pants. "I don't believe I have, no. Do you know what her question was about?"

I told her what little I knew about Ursula. She lived in Massachusetts, worked at a quilt museum there.

"Lowell?" Nan asked.

I felt a ray of hope. I'd piqued her interest.

"I sort of remember an e-mail about a shuttle from the people there. God, I wish my brain worked better." Her forehead was creased with the effort to recall.

"Can you access your e-mail from here? Do you keep the files?"

Nan held up a hand. "Slow down, I don't do anything with my e-mail except read it. I've got a son who handles all that."

I gave up when it was obvious Nan didn't remember any more about her discussion with Ursula, but I was on the right track. The sewing tool could have been at the quilt museum. Ursula had e-mailed the expert, questioning her about a sewing tool she'd found.

TWENTY-TWO

I left the service after another hour. Stories about Mercedes were just getting started. Each tale sparked another quilter's memory and the line to get to the microphone had grown. It was going to be a long night. I was ready for bed. Tired, beyond tired. Exhausted. My head hurt.

I was no closer to finding Ursula. She hadn't had the nerve to show up and tell her story about Mercedes.

I had just passed the street lamp by the Pirates' Den when I realized someone was behind me. I whirled, and was relieved to see Quentin Rousseau scurrying behind me.

"Dewey," he called. I waited for him to catch up. The night had turned cloudy without much ambient light. The trees were very dark.

"Man, am I glad it's you," I said, regulating my heart beat, slowing to normal. Thank goodness it wasn't Paul.

"Nice job on the memorial," I said. "You really pulled that together quickly."

"I'm glad I found you," he said. He was panting a little bit. "Kym asked me to tell you she needs you."

That stopped me. "Why would she want *me?*"

He shook his head. "I don't know. She asked me to bring you to her."

She had her nerve. She was the last person I wanted to see. She probably had a computer crisis. "I don't have time right now."

Quentin was not to be put off that easily. "You should make time for your family," he said sternly.

I turned to leave.

"Do you have brothers or sisters, Quentin?" I asked.

He shook his head. It figured. He was one of those only children who romanticized the idea of siblings. He didn't want to hear anything about the reality of trying to get along with them. Especially grown ones and the women they marry.

I looked at him. His face was perspiring. Kym must have convinced him this was life or death. "Let me tell you something. Drama is my sister-in-law's middle name, Quentin. She's not happy unless she's stirring the pot."

His voice deepened, and he growled, "Come with me, Dewey. Now."

Something had shifted. He didn't sound like the easy-going guy Freddy'd introduced me to. I glanced up. We had walked away from Merrill Hall, away from the other buildings. The entire conference was inside at Mercedes' memorial, hearing testimonials about the woman who'd brought them together. Buster and Tony were off stalking their own prey.

He was pointing a gun at my midsection. I felt the muzzle graze my arm, and every hair stood on end.

My mind couldn't catch up with the change in him. What was he doing? I looked down at the gun and up at him. I couldn't compute what was happening.

Quentin's agenda had changed. I had a sinking feeling I wasn't going to like what he had planned.

I forced myself to look at the gun. I'd had guns pointed at me before. It was never a good feeling, but like most things in life, facing it head on was better than ignoring it.

Hold on. I'd seen that piece before. I let out a long, slow exhale. My whole body relaxed, giving me a sick sensation as the adrenaline dissipated.

I said, "Did you take that from Mercedes? That gun's not real."

I took a step away. I was getting away from this nut job as soon as I could. I thought about Tony and Buster, hiding in the woods, tracking a four-legged monster. I needed to get away from this two-legged one. Quickly.

But Quentin poked me again, hard and laughed. An evil laugh. "Not real? Why don't you ask Mercedes about that? I think the bullet that killed her was very real."

He leaned in, his breath on my neck causing me to shudder. I tumbled to the truth. Mercedes had pulled a real gun on Paul, and then Quentin had used it against her. That's why the fake one in her room had never been found.

My mouth went dry. "What do you want?"

"The Rose Box complete, that's what I want. And I will do anything to get it."

He tightened his grip on my arm. A squeal of pain slipped through my lips.

"You've been very clever, so far, Ms. Pellicano. You figured out that the Rose Sewing Box was the true treasure."

Talking was not killing. I'd keep him talking while I figured out what to do next. "I saw it in Mercedes' room before she was killed. It was gone afterward. Stands to reason that it was the prize."

"But you didn't tell the police you'd seen it. That was your major mistake. You thought you knew who'd killed her, but you didn't take into account that the box was missing, too. You overlooked that in your zeal to get Paul Wiggins."

"Not exactly."

"I know that tool is here somewhere. You seem to be the connecting thread as well as the erstwhile sleuth, so I'm going to let you do the work for me."

"I don't know where it is." I wasn't going to tell him I knew who had the sewing bird. Ursula.

"Find it."

"Where do you suggest I look for it?"

"That's up to you. You have two hours."

"And why would I do this?"

"I'll show you."

He pointed down a set of concrete steps cut into the hillside that I hadn't noticed before. We went down two flights into an underground parking garage. A bright red PT Cruiser with a license plate holder that read "Quilters Do It on Every Block" was right in front of me, mocking me.

The garage walls were painted bright blue. Low light came from overhead fixtures. The place was deserted. With all the quilter's car keys still in Kym's possession, the parking garage was sure to be the last place anyone was coming tonight.

From here we entered a low-ceiling room marked "Utilities." Quentin unlocked the door and pulled it open with a loud crack. He nudged me into the room and the door slammed behind me. It was completely dark. My breath caught. I could feel the cold seeping from the underground walls.

Quentin moved me forward, pushing the gun at my back. I gasped as I felt the barrel in the small of my back, a crawling sensation moving up as though the uninvited nudge was too much to bear.

I loved when Buster touched me there, when we were out in a crowd. Just a gentle finger right above my waistline, where my back curved inward. The little stroke made me feel safe and secure, and loved. A little hello. I'm by your side. A gentle reminder that he was with me.

This felt like a cruel parody of my lover's touch. I fought not to shiver in fright, feeling my teeth ache from holding myself in check. I swallowed hard, grateful he was behind me and couldn't see how difficult it was to complete the swallow. I had no saliva.

I tripped over something, and nearly fell. I gasped. Quentin steadied me.

Over my own frightened exhales, I heard

breathing. An irrational fright, visceral and ancient, tore through my body. Something was in here, alive. A picture of the mountain lion passed through my brain, overloading my already taxed nervous system. Tears sprang to my eyes. I didn't dare wipe them away.

Quentin turned on a lantern. The light was low and took several minutes to reach the inner recesses of the room. The walls were lined with gray utility shelving. I'd bumped into a yellow bucket on wheels with a huge string mop stuffed into it.

The light reached into the recesses of the room. Finally, I saw what was breathing so hard.

A blindfolded Kym was curled in the corner on a cot, her breathing erratic and shallow. A sleeping bag was at her feet. Her hands were tied behind her. I started toward her, but Quentin jerked me back.

"Stay put," he said. "She's fine. And she'll remain okay as long as you deliver the goods."

"Let me straighten her out. Cover her up at least. She looks uncomfortable." I wanted to touch her. My brother would be so upset to see her like this.

"She's sedated. Don't worry about her."

He jerked my arm roughly, turning me

around. His breath was rank. I took a step back, and he squeezed. Hard. I grunted with the effort of trying to break away from him. The place where Ursula had hit me throbbed.

"You've got to give me some time, Quentin. I'm not up to speed on this one. I thought Paul killed Mercedes, remember?"

He laughed — a shrill laugh that cut my spine in half. I felt my knees buckle. He let go of me, and I leaned against the wall for support. The cold concrete helped bring me back to the present.

Quentin kicked, sending an empty Diet Coke can skittering across the floor. The noise was tiny in the space.

"That bitch! I wasn't out to kill anyone, just to get back what was mine. I never should have confided in Mercedes. She knew what I needed. She knew I would pay to get it back. She just didn't know when to stop pushing."

Mercedes was a pushy broad, there was no doubt about that.

"The Rose Box is my heritage. My father was a gambler, a wastrel. He sold everything of value that we'd ever owned, including anything that was precious to my mother, including her collection of sewing kits. I've spent the last four years gathering what I could, off eBay and at quilt shows. I've traveled this country from coast to coast. My mother is a broken woman, devastated that her family's heirlooms have been scattered."

His eyes unfocused. "That sewing bird is the final piece. The last thing I needed."

I was not dealing with a sane man. My mind kept repeating the word "Nutso" over and over again. I shook my head to stop the loop.

"You've got two hours. I'll keep Kym alive until one o'clock this morning," he said.

"Why then?" Two hours wasn't much time.

"The cleaning crew starts work again by six. Do you want them to find your sister's dead body?"

"Sister-in-law," I said automatically. I was scanning the room, trying to find a way out. There was none. No windows. No way out except the door we'd just come through. No one would hear us. It was a concrete room, in the underground parking structure.

"Find the sewing bird, give it to me, and I will let Kym go free. If you go to the police, I will kill Kym and disappear. I want that sewing bird and the complete set, but not enough to ruin my life," he said. "Your clock is ticking. Go."

"I need to make sure she's okay first," I said.

He looked at me, assessing my intention. He opened the door and let me go in. He didn't look at Kym. He'd already shifted to treating her as though she was a thing, an object that could be dispensed with as needed. That meant he was truly dangerous.

Kym raised her head. Her chest was heaving and I could hear the wheeze in her throat. She was having trouble breathing. Without her inhaler, she was in danger of having an asthma attack. That wouldn't be good.

Her skin looked awful, the blisters watery and white. the allergic reaction had intensified. She tried to focus on me.

"Dewey," she croaked.

My heart hurt at the pitiful sight of her.

"Your soap cure made me worse," she said.

Of course, blame me. I laughed, a bitter sound. "Oh, Kym. You'll never change."

"My throat keeps closing up. My lungs hurt. I need my inhaler," she said in short bursts.

"I'll get it and bring it to you," I promised.

"No, you won't," Quentin said from outside the room. The acoustics in here were such that he could hear us whispering. I frowned at Kym and patted her hand, in what I'd hoped was a reassuring manner.

"Tony?" she croaked.

"Sssh," I said. Quentin knew Tony was my brother, but he didn't need to be reminded in this moment that I had a law enforcement connection. He needed to believe that I would get what he needed, so he could escape and let Kym go.

Quentin grabbed me and pulled me away. Kym's head lolled and her eyes closed. She was out again.

Quentin said, "Your sister-in-law will be unconscious for another hour or so. You don't want to know what will happen to Kym if you're late."

I bristled under his touch, but he was strong for a little guy. His forearms were ropy from hours of quilting and he pulled me into him.

"Don't fuck this up. I didn't want to kill Mercedes. I wouldn't have had to shoot if she'd just stuck to our agreement. I had her cash, but she wanted more."

I felt a twinge of sadness. Mercedes' greed had killed her.

Quentin said, "I don't want to kill again. Find the Rose bird and bring it back to me, and nothing will happen to your beloved sister-in-law."

He pushed me out the door. I stood in the parking garage, panting, trying to regain the regular rhythm of my breathing.

My beloved sister-in-law? Dude had the wrong Pellicano, but I was the only one who could save her.

Buster and Tony would be gone all night. There was no chance I'd find either one of them before the deadline. I was on my own.

Twenty-Three

I raced up the steps and outside.

A deer raised her head at my appearance, assessing the threat I posed. My danger was out of sight, but still very present and scary. Kym was being held in a hidden chamber underneath Asilomar. Still, the pine trees swayed in the wind, wild flowers bloomed in the grass. Beyond, I could see the ocean and knew that it was sending wave after wave onto the sand, relentless and unstoppable. Like Quentin.

I tried to clear the cobwebs that fear was setting up in my brain. I needed to be hyper-alert, like the deer, attuned to danger on the wind. She put her head back down, assuming I wouldn't hurt her. I wished I could return to normal so easily.

Now what? I'd been looking for Ursula ever since I saw her yesterday. She'd not been where I'd thought she was. How was I going to find her in two hours?

I gathered my bearings. This parking garage was not the one that Buster had parked in the other night. This one was closer to the Stuck-up Inn. I fought the urge to go back to my room and pull the covers over my head, but Kym would be lost if I did that.

I'd seen Ursula last at the Pirates' Den. I headed back there. The staff would be around to lock the doors at midnight.

Most of the group was still at Merrill Hall, just a few hundred yards to the north. I could see the lights and hear the tinkle of piano music. A huge laugh went up. The memorial for Mercedes was going strong.

I entered the living room and closed the door, feeling its weight as I shut out the rest of the world.

I looked around the room. I'd seen Lucy's pictures from her grandfather's album. Back then, the dorm had been one large room, with bunk beds laid out next to each other. The space was used to its maximum. When the state took over, in the fifties, the rooms had been completely remodeled. Walls had been put up to divide the rooms into smaller sleeping rooms with the privacy that tourists or conventioneers would require.

Ursula had been in here. She'd had the

sewing bird and laid it on my fabric. I pictured how it might have happened. I breathed in, letting the salty, slightly musty air fill my lungs.

I knew she'd been near the table by the window, where I'd left my fabric. She'd opened the curtain, letting the sun shine in, at least for the few minutes needed to expose my fabric. Why?

Mercedes had had her meeting with Quentin downstairs in her room. Ursula waited above in the living room. That didn't feel right. Why would Ursula wait out here in the open? This room was always unlocked during the day. Anyone could have walked in on her. Paul could have walked in on her.

She had to be hiding, at least for part of the time she was waiting for Quentin and Mercedes to need her. She had to be available, ready to join them and hand over the sewing bird.

Mercedes wouldn't want Ursula to know she was hitting Quentin up for more money, so she kept Ursula out of sight until she was finished. I could imagine something got Ursula's attention and she came out and looked out the window, laying the sewing bird on my fabric. She'd not found out what was going on.

I was sure she hadn't heard a shot, or if

she had, she mistook it for a car backfiring or a branch cracking. A .22 like the one Mercedes had made a very small noise. If the lunch bell had been ringing or the ravens squawking, Ursula could have easily heard nothing.

I tried to picture Mercedes' room below me. The living room was on the hillside. Her room was not directly below the living room because of the slope. I went into the short hall that led to the bathroom. Now I was directly over her room. I went into the bathroom stall. The walls were concrete block; there was no access to the downstairs.

I walked back into the living room. The closet was over the space that Mercedes' room occupied. I opened the closet door and went in, banging on the walls. Had Ursula hidden in here all day? That would be majorly uncomfortable.

How was Mercedes going to signal to Ursula that it was time for her to show up with the bird?

I thought about the walkie-talkies Kevin had gotten one Christmas. He sent me into all of the rooms of the house, into the attic and the crawlspace that served as a basement. Reception was not great. Technology was vastly improved now, but I hadn't seen any evidence of Mercedes having one.

I went outside. There was a small window that was up high in the wall, like a basement window. I peered inside, but could see nothing. It looked like it should have been part of the room that Mercedes had stayed in, but with the slope of the hill, it was hard to tell.

I went back inside. I had to think harder. Faster. Ursula had seemed to appear in the room. She hadn't entered by the door that I'd gone through. So where had she come from?

I tired to picture where I'd first seen her. It was in the corner. I knocked on the wall, trying to hear if there was a dead space. I found the closet door, and opened it. It was too dark to see anything.

I opened the door wide, trying to get light into the small space. I grabbed the desk lamp, and used it to illuminate the dark. I tapped my foot on the floor, stomping and listening. The floor gave the same hollow sound, until suddenly it didn't.

I tapped again. There was dead air beneath the far end of the closet. I got on my hands and knees and rubbed my hands along the worn floor. A splinter worked its way into the meaty part of my thumb, and I stopped to suck it out.

As I sat back on my haunches, my foot hit

something hard. I turned and spotted a wrought iron handle on the floor.

I pulled on it. Nothing.

I felt with my fingers. There was an area about four feet square where the boards of the floor had been scribed. I moved away, being careful not to stand in that area.

I pulled again. The four-foot section of floor came up in my hands. With it open, I could see something leading into the space below.

I wished I had a flashlight. I listened. I couldn't hear anything in the space. It was completely dark, like going down a tunnel.

I reached my hand through, trying to feel for a way down. I felt the top rung of a crude wooden ladder.

This had to lead to Ursula. A picture of Kym in another dark, dank space flitted through my mind. I lowered myself onto the first rung and tentatively took a step.

My heart beat unmercifully. My breath caught. I had no idea what was beneath me. This was torture.

Before I could think any more, I scrambled down the ladder. I was always in favor of ripping off the band-aid. Kevin preferred the slower way.

At the bottom, I stopped. I could hear my own breath sounding like I'd just run the

Rock 'n' Roll marathon. I forced myself to quiet, holding my breath and let it out slowly through my nose.

I heard a gasp. My heart did a flip.

A light flickered and then came on.

Ursula sat up in a twin bed that took up most of the wall opposite me. The room was small, maybe six feet square. The walls had been wallpapered a long time ago in a classic William Morris pattern that had been popular a hundred years ago.

"Jesus! Dewey!"

Ursula was shaking. She pulled the covers up to her neck, fingers twitching. The bed was covered in a wildly colorful crazy quilt, very much like the cape she'd been wearing on the cliffs on Tuesday morning.

I'd found Ursula's lair.

The room was sparsely furnished. Just a small writing desk that held a sewing machine, a three-drawer wooden dresser. No closet, no bathroom. The window high above the bed was the one I'd seen from outside earlier.

"This is where you live while you're at Asilomar?" I asked in disbelief. As sanctuaries go, it was one step above the Underground Railroad shelters I'd seen in historical homes back east.

She looked around the room. "It's lovely.

You don't know what it means to have a place of my own."

Even if it was a dingy room, walled off and forgotten.

"How?" I asked. My legs felt rubbery, and I leaned against the ladder I just descended.

"Mercedes gives me the money that Paul pays her for the conference."

Paul Wiggins was such a creep. What did you have to do to a woman to make her feel like her best shot at a life was one week a year in a room no better than a cell? Jail comes in all forms. This felt to her like freedom.

"She doesn't charge me much for this."

Good ole Mercedes. Making sure she got her cut. I couldn't believe she made Ursula pay anything for these accommodations.

But I had another woman trapped in a jail of sorts that I needed to rescue.

"Ursula, I've come for the sewing bird."

"What?" she said, her fingers had stopped convulsing and color was returning to her face. "You can't have it. It's my ticket out of here," she said

"Where is it?" I said. I straightened, trying to recover a more powerful position. Ursula sat up higher, tossing the quilt off her shoulders, and putting her feet into hard-soled slippers that were under her bed. She stood, too. She was wearing gray sweatpants and a matching shirt. No pretty pajamas for her. She must always be prepared to flee.

She shook her head. "I can't tell you."

"Paul is looking for you. He wonders where you are," I said. I didn't want to threaten her with her husband, but I needed some leverage. "Do you want me to tell him where you are?"

Her face pinched. The wrinkles around her mouth told me this was a familiar expression. Pinched and scared. I felt sick at how much my words had frightened her. It was an empty threat. I needed the sewing bird, but I couldn't sacrifice her to get it.

"It's hidden," she whispered. "You've got to give me time to get away. I'll really kill myself this time."

I doubted that. Whatever strength she'd pulled on through the years was enough to keep her sane and healthy even while married to a psychopath. Why would she give up her life now? Now that it was about to change so much.

I paced the length of her room. What was I going to do to protect her? And get Kym?

An old treadle sewing machine was set up in the corner. I'd heard about these machines, requiring no electrical power, running on pedal power. I turned on another gas lamp that sat next to it and looked at what she was working on. More crazy blocks. Strips of fabrics and muslin squares lay on the sewing machine bed. Several finished blocks were laid out. The fabrics were sewn willy-nilly with a randomness that was appealing. She'd been using silks, and their sheen was dazzling.

The crazy block was her block of choice.

Ursula should have been safe in her own home, but she was not. We're searched at the airports, we're wiretapped. The politicians worry us about our borders, from the terrorists without — but for Ursula, the terror was behind her front door. Her home was not a sanctuary. Just the opposite. The only peace she got was once a year at this quilt retreat. Seven days out of three hundred sixty-five.

I picked up a block and examined it. The fabrics were slippery smooth. Her cape had been made of many of these hodge-podge blocks. It seemed like there was no order to them, no rhyme or reason. The pieces were large and small, three-sided, five-sided. It didn't matter. Somehow they worked together and formed a cohesive whole.

These were the pieces of Ursula's life held together with thread. Chaotic, but beautiful.

She spoke quietly. "He'd stopped beating me three years ago."

I looked up in surprise. "He stopped hitting you? So why leave him now?" I asked.

She sat heavily on the bed, looking into the distance. I followed her gaze but could see nothing. She was lost in her own world. A place I couldn't follow her.

"It was worse than being hit."

She didn't say any more. Finally I said, "I don't get it."

Her voice was small. She picked up the pillow on her bed, and hugged it, pulling it close to her heart.

"I don't know if I can make you understand," she buried her face in the down.

"Try," I said.

She gnawed on the side of her thumb. "It wasn't all bad, you know. After he'd beat me, he was so sorry. He'd leave me alone for a few months. During that time, he was sweet and caring, the best husband anyone could want."

Her face softened, the lines around her mouth disappearing. Her forehead smoothed, and her hands clasped her elbows. She looked pretty as she thought about the good times in her life.

She closed her eyes, as though she didn't want to see what was coming. "Then the cycle would start again. It would always begin in the same way, with him growing short and impatient about little things. I fed the fish too much. I opened the window when there was pollen outside. I closed the window. Didn't I know he needed a cross breeze? I could tell when he was building up a head of steam. A laundry list of my failings as a wife. And I knew what was coming next. A beating."

She was so matter of fact. *And then he'd beat me.*

I tried to imagine Buster laying his hands on me in any way but a loving manner. His hands that loved me, tickled me, teased me, brought me happiness over and over again. I pictured myself arm-in-arm with him, walking down the street, knowing that that fist would be raised against me, but I couldn't do it.

Ursula said, "I knew that was the way it worked. I put up with it. I was willing to take the good with the bad."

She pushed the pillow away. She saw I wasn't getting it. "You can handle anything as long as it's consistent. But about three years ago, after I'd been coming here alone for years without attending class, he just stopped."

I held my breath. That could have been

the beginning of a new life for her.

"We never talked about it. For months I waited for the familiar pattern to emerge. The holidays were always a tense time in our household, but Thanksgiving and Christmas passed without incidents."

That was good, I thought.

She rubbed her stomach as though she had a tummy ache that wouldn't stop throbbing. I wondered about her broken body. How many aches and pains she must have, remnants from the brutality. How jeopardized her health was. How much life did she have left?

"At first, it was great. I went out to work for the first time in years. I started working in a shop, making pattern samples. I volunteered at the quilt museum."

I felt my own stomach tense as though I knew a blow was coming. Mercedes had wanted to keep us secure at Asilomar. It was too late now. No one was safe. Kym was locked up by Quentin. Safety was an illusion.

"As time passed and he still didn't hit me, the anticipation got worse. I could never let my guard down. I was sure he was going to beat me again. I couldn't concentrate on quilting. I was like a dam, ready to burst.

"I began to wish he would give me a beating. I was always girded against that moment, but it never came.

"For the first time in my life, I was having a life outside my house, outside my one week in Asilomar a year."

Her world had been so small.

"And I began to worry about losing it. When it was just me and Paul, I had nothing to compare my life to. I'd left home at eighteen and married Paul and spent the next thirty years living my life at his whim."

"So maybe he's a changed man." If I believed people could change, Paul had to have that chance too. I'd thought he was a murderer, but Quentin had put the lie to that.

"The longer it went on, I wanted to believe that. I'd heard that older men change. They lose testosterone and they mellow. The rages of his youth might be over."

She looked up at me, her eyes sad. "But I couldn't enjoy anything, just waiting. It was horrible. My life, as I knew it, was over."

Her voice changed, became more animated. "Last year, here, I asked Mercedes to help me get out. She said she knew people. She'd help me find a safe place, far away from Paul, far away from his fists. The threats, the not knowing. All I had to do was get some money together."

Her voice fell again as she relived the torture that was her life. "I had no way of doing that. Paul still monitored my cell, my e-mails, my credit cards. I had no money of my own except for the little money I made at the quilt shop. That wasn't going to be enough to start over."

I fingered one of the blocks, feeling the ridges and bumps caused by the seams coming together. I didn't dare say a word. Ursula was lost in her story.

"Then Mercedes told me about a sewing tool laying forgotten in the drawers in the back room of the quilt museum. No one would ever miss it. The museum receives so much stuff from well-meaning people, they don't have time to catalogue everything. It was in a bin with other sewing implements, yet to be inventoried."

Finally, the sewing bird.

"She would pay me ten thousand dollars for it."

"She was buying it for Quentin?" I asked.

She nodded. "He'd been looking for the Rose Box and the missing piece for years. Mercedes knew Nan had the box. Quentin was willing to pay fifty thousand dollars."

But that hadn't been enough for Mercedes.

"It was surprisingly easy to steal. I put it in my purse during one of my docent tours. Mercedes was right, no one cared about it."

She was silent for a moment.

"How did she die?" she asked quietly. She wanted me to let her off the hook.

I said, "My guess is that she told Quentin she wanted more money. She probably threatened him with her gun, like she did Paul, but instead Quentin used it against her."

I shuddered at the idea that I'd been holding a loaded gun and hadn't realized it.

Ursula looked as though she might throw up.

I said, "Quentin was looking for the bird. The room was trashed. He'd torn the place apart. Didn't you hear him? Didn't you hear the shot?"

She shook her head. "I can't hear much. There's a wall with the plumbing for the bathrooms between my room and hers. My only exit was the way you just came down. Mercedes would knock on the floor of the closet to let me know the coast was clear. I'd come up, and use the bathroom at night when no one was around. Once every couple of days, I'd shower in her room."

"No one knew you were here? Not even Kym?" I asked.

"Lord, no. It was just between Mercedes and I. She'd discovered this room one year and decided I could use it."

"And that day? The day she was killed? You didn't hear *anything?*"

She shook her head. "After a while, I went up into the living room. I looked out the window, but I couldn't see anything."

That was when she'd laid the sewing bird down on my blueprint fabric. The open curtain had let in enough light to expose the image onto my piece.

I said, "Give me the sewing bird."

"I don't have it."

My heart sunk like a stone in the ocean. I felt myself go cold. A picture of Kym, helpless, lifeless crossed my mind and I felt myself curl up in pain.

"I have to have the sewing bird. Quentin has my sister-in-law. He wants that tool."

Ursula was shaking her head slowly from side to side. "I'm sorry. I feel for your sister-in-law, I do, but I gave the bird to Mercedes."

I pictured Kym as she was right now, tied up in that dingy room. She would be so unhappy when she woke up and realized that she hadn't washed her hair today. Her fingernails were probably cracked, and her lip gloss nowhere to be found. I couldn't imagine how itchy she would be after a night without her medication.

I'd often wanted to shut Kym up, and gagging her had often crossed my mind when we'd worked together at QP. This was beyond anything even I'd imagined for Kym, and I'd come up with some pretty exotic tortures when she worked for me. I'd once envisioned her buried under a shipment of batting, and would have gladly sewed her mouth shut many times.

The last thing I wanted was for Kevin to see his wife like that. Or worse. If she didn't get out . . . that wouldn't happen. I couldn't let that happen.

"I don't believe you," I said.

She thinned her lips, her body shaking from the effort of not telling me where the bird was. Her eyes gave her away, straying to the dresser against the wall.

I walked the several steps to the dresser and pulled out a drawer, dumping the contents on the floor. Several bras and panties fell to the floor. Ursula gasped.

"Where is it?" I yelled. "Tell me."

She clutched the pillow to her. She acted as though I was hitting her. I felt sick to my stomach.

I yelled, "Do you realize Quentin will kill you? He's not going to give up. This bird is more to him than a collectible, it's a family heirloom. A lost legacy that means more to him than life. Especially your life."

I pulled open the second drawer, pulling out the T-shirts and jeans that occupied it. I ran my hand around the inside to make sure it was empty. I turned the drawer over. Ursula grunted as though in pain.

"You'll spend the rest of your life running from two men, Paul and Quentin. Let me help you, Ursula. You can create a life worth living. You can be happy."

She began to weep.

The third drawer fell forward too easily and I knew it held the prize. I upended it, her pieces of fabric, thread, and scissors falling to the floor. Taped on the back was the sewing bird, the weight making the drawer top heavy.

I ripped away the duct tape that held it to the underside. The sewing bird that held the key to Kym's safety dropped into my hand. A great wave of relief washed over me.

TWENTY-FOUR

I sat on the bed next to Ursula and rubbed her arm. She leaned away from me.

I pulled her to her feet. "Let me help you get out of here. My car is the red Honda in the lot next door. You can't miss it. It has a QP sign on the side."

I gave her my car keys.

"Take my car."

I scribbled my address on a scrap of paper. "Go to my house in San Jose. That other key will open the back door. Go. We'll figure out what to do with you later. Just get out of town. Away from Paul and Quentin."

She made up her mind and scrambled up the ladder, faster than I thought a woman her age could move. I followed her, and we both dashed outside. She went to the parking lot.

I had fifteen minutes on Quentin's deadline. I dialed Buster's cell and got the same message, the caller was not available. Tony must have taken him well into the woods, looking for the mountain lion's lair. He was having a wonderful time, backpacking with my brother while I needed him here. I felt a surge of anger at both of them. Kym was Tony's sister-in-law, too. Buster was best friends with Kevin. Why weren't they around when I needed them?

I shook off the self-pity.

I had only a few minutes before it was time to meet Quentin and trade this silly sewing tool for my sister-in-law. If it meant he got away with killing Mercedes, there was nothing I could do about it.

The leaves on the trees were dripping with fog. The overhead telephone lines were humming. The fog disguised the outlines of the buildings, softening edges and blurring the angles of the trees. A huge raven landed in front of me, startling me. She pulled at the edges of a potato chip bag and raced away as I approached. Gulls' cries sounded sadder than ever.

Quentin was waiting for me at the door to the maintenance room.

"I want to see Kym," I told Quentin.

"No. You're going to have to take my word that she's okay," he said.

I stood my ground. "Not good enough."

317

"She said to tell you to hurry up because her hair is frizzing in the fog."

That was proof she was alive. I nearly laughed. She was alive and not too frightened to worry about her looks.

"Where's the sewing bird?" he demanded.

I ignored his question. I had to maintain some control over the conversation. "Do you have the Rose Box here?" I asked. "Shouldn't we make sure the tool fits in it?"

"I know it's the right tool. Hand it over. I need to be on my way back to New Orleans."

He looked at his watch. "My car is due here in five minutes."

"Well I guess it wasn't about the money, then."

"It's always been about family honor, Dewey. Something you don't know much about."

I bristled. "Really?" I'd risked my neck for a sister-in-law I didn't really care too much for. Who was this guy to tell me about family honor?

Kym made a noise from the other room that sounded suspiciously like a fake cry. She wasn't moved by Quentin's story. And she didn't believe in mollycoddling kidnappers. Quentin must have had a rough night.

"I'll give you the sewing bird, but you've

318

got to untie Kym first."

"Why would I do that?"

"Because she and I are going to get out of here as you promised."

"How do I know you have it?"

I pulled the piece of blueprint fabric out of my pocket. "See that?" I asked. "That is the shape of the sewing bird, right?"

He took the fabric and held it under a light. "Looks like it," he said.

Kym moaned again. "Let me out of here, you piece of shit," she cried, from the other room.

I tensed. Quentin squeezed his eyes shut. Kym had not rested quietly. She was getting on his last nerve. I had to be sure he didn't shoot her just to shut her up.

"Let's just get Kym out of here," I said. "She can leave. You've got me. I've got the bird. Let her go."

He seemed to like that idea. He unlocked the door. He had moved Kym to a chair while I was gone. Her face was red and there were bags under her eyes, but she looked more mad now than in fear of her life.

"Get me out of here, Dewey."

Of course this was my fault.

"Working on it, Kym," I muttered. "Try to keep yourself together for a few more minutes."

"Hurry up," Quentin said with a new urgency. I glanced over to see the gun pointed at us.

Kym's bravado disappeared. She slumped in her seat. I kicked her chair leg to get her attention.

I whispered in Kym's ear. "Just get outside and run for help. I'll be right behind you."

She nodded.

"You untie her," Quentin said. "Quickly. I'm losing patience here."

I worked on the knots he'd made — knots that had gotten tighter as Kym struggled against them in the night.

Kym leaned around to see what I was doing. Her moving just made the knots twist together tighter.

"Hold still," I said, through gritted teeth. "I nearly have it. Get ready to run."

Her arms came loose. Her sigh whistled through gritted teeth as she rubbed her upper arms briskly. Her blisters looked worse and her breathing was labored.

Quentin was muttering, "Hurry up, hurry up."

I pulled out the final knot. Kym jumped up. I stepped away from her, giving her room. She staggered. The chair fell back with a clatter.

I turned to Quentin. "Outside," I said.

"That was not the deal," he said.

Kym took several steps and collapsed between us. "My legs," she said, as she went down.

I grabbed her arm as she fell but she slithered to the floor as though her bones had turned to jelly in the night. "She needs fresh air," I said.

"Damn it!" Quentin said. He raised the gun as though he was going to strike Kym with it.

Quentin loomed over us, standing in front of the open door. I jumped in front of Kym, shielding her from the gun. "No," I yelled.

My cry was interrupted by the appearance of Paul Wiggins in the doorway behind Quentin. I blinked, not quite believing my eyes. What was he doing here?

"Everything okay, Dewey?" Paul said, his eyes looking from Kym on the floor to me, hanging on to her one limp arm, to Quentin holding a gun by its butt, high in the air. Paul's eyes widened.

Quentin was completely discombobulated at the sound of a new voice. He wheeled and flipped the gun around.

And shot.

The noise inside the small concrete room was deafening. Kym screamed, her hands over her ears. I grabbed her, dragging her out of the room and into the parking garage. I pushed her toward the steps. I took her hand and made it grab the metal railing.

"Drag your ass up those steps," I said, giving her a push. "Go."

There was another shot. I looked back.

Quentin was staring at Paul who was on the ground, not moving. I could see a small hole in his forehead. There was blood on his chest.

He looked at me and I could see the murderous intent in his eyes. I grabbed the mop bucket, and pushed it at him as hard as I could. The wheels caught on the uneven concrete and wobbled. I kicked out, catching the bucket full force. This time it moved, and slammed in to Quentin at the knees. He went down, the gun firing in the air.

I raced to the stairs, finding Kym about half way up and pulling her the rest of the way.

At the top of the stairs, I took a breath. The gunshots seemed to be still reverberating in the night air. The dew was heavy, fog moving in. I felt the moisture gather on the hair on my arms. Proof I was still alive. For now.

I looked at the stairwell. Quentin would be coming up any moment. I looked for a hiding place. A sheltering oak tree stood in front of us.

"You feeling your legs yet?" I asked Kym.

"Yes, they're tingling like crazy. They hurt," she said, on the verge of tears.

I searched the area. "There's a low branch over there. We can climb up and hide from him." It was a crappy plan. I'd have to pull Kym up the tree. But the branch was low and we might be hidden long enough for Quentin to miss us.

"Move, move, move."

I shoved Kym toward the tree, looking back to see where Quentin was. When I looked ahead of me again, my heart stopped.

There was a mountain lion lying in the tree, on the branch I'd told Kym to grab onto.

"Hold on," I said.

"Dewey, quit it. I'm trying," her voice trailed off to a sob. "I can barely feel my legs. They're asleep," she said.

Kym began to sink to the ground, her hands splayed out in front of her. Looking four-legged. Exactly the position Tony had warned us about.

"Get up," I hissed, pulling on her, keeping one eye on the lion in the tree. The lion was watching us as if she was bored.

Kym was dead weight, still groggy from the drugs Quentin had given her. I yelled in her ear. "Right now. Get up! Make yourself large!"

The lion growled tentatively as if deciding if we were worth a meal. The sound was bone-chilling. I grabbed at Kym, forcing her up against the tree trunk like a rag doll. I used one hand to hold her there. With the other I reached for the sewing bird. If I threw it as hard as I could and hit the cat right between the eyes . . .

I looked up. The cat's eyes were golden and mesmerizing, seeming to glow in the dark. I couldn't raise my arm.

Kym was fighting me, shoving at my hand with her arm, twisting her body away. Her breath was labored. "Get off me. I can't breathe," she said, desperate to break free. I leaned against her. Her body smelled rank.

I heard the screech of the door I'd been waiting to hear. Quentin was on his way out. I couldn't let him walk into this.

"Mountain lion, Quentin!" I yelled.

Quentin came out of the stairwell and looked around to see where my voice was coming from. He caught sight of Kym and started our way. He moved quickly, but stumbled, his feet getting caught in the roots of the tree. He lost his footing and went down on all fours.

"Stand up!" I yelled at him.

It was not enough. Quentin didn't seem to hear me over his panting.

As if in slow motion, I watched the giant cat leap from her perch in the tree and land on Quentin's head. Kym screamed and turned away, hugging the tree.

The lion snarled and I could hear the vicious roar as she tore open his throat. I raised my hand as if to hit the mountain lion, realizing in a second how futile my attempt would be. I needed something bigger. A branch, a rock. I bent over, hands scrabbling on the ground, trying to find something.

Over my head, a shot rang out. The mountain lion collapsed in a heap on top of Quentin.

Tony was standing ten feet away, lowering his rifle. Buster was next to him with his service gun still pointed at the heaving animal.

The lion gave one last breath and shuddered. Quentin didn't move, his blood pooling around his back and trickling downhill gathering in the dirt beneath a mountain laurel.

Kym slipped to the ground, her back against the tree trunk, screaming. Buster dropped his hand and in two strides had wrapped his free arm around me, the other still holding his gun. Tony bent over Kym, calming her. Tony's voice was soothing and Kym quieted into gulps.

Buster was breathing hard in my ear. My feet were off the ground. I sunk into his chest. I felt my heart synch with his, and finally slow down.

"Okay?" he said. He could barely get the word out. I felt a tear drip from his chin down my neck.

I nodded. My voice was gone. I clutched the sewing bird in my free hand. We clung to each other.

Kym finally quieted. Tony handed her his cell phone. He must have gotten Kevin out of bed because soon Kym was chattering a mile a minute. She would be okay. Kevin would see to that.

"I saw you. I saw the lion leap," Buster said. "I really thought you were a goner." His voice caught and he buried his face in my hair. I squeezed his neck tighter.

"I'm fine," I said.

"You better stay that way."

Tony leaned over the lion and Quentin. He checked Quentin's pulse, even though it was obvious he'd bled out. His neck was a reddened mess of tissue and sinew.

"Is he dead?" I asked.

"They both are," Tony said.

"It's too bad such a beautiful animal had to die," I said to Buster.

"There's only one thing I care about and that's you," he said. He pulled me in closer.

"What about Kym?" I said, teasing.

"I'm glad she's okay, but you are the most important thing in my world."

TWENTY-FIVE

"Are you finished? What do you think?"

Cinnamon interrupted my thoughts and I startled. She put a hand on my arm and I smiled at her. I wasn't as fragile as she thought.

"No, not finished. It needs a little something else."

"You'll figure it out. Unloosen your mind," she said. She moved away to answer a student's question. Unloosen my mind. I tried.

It was Friday afternoon. I was in the classroom, with Cinnamon, Lucy and a few others. Harriet and many of the quilters had gone home early after last night's traumatic end.

My quilt was mostly finished. I took a step back. I'd used my photos to create appliqués of Merrill Hall and the Chapel. The middle of the quilt consisted of a semi-realistic view of Asilomar, although the rustic buildings were crowded together. I'd filled in with tall pines and a view of the ocean. But something was missing.

Lucy came up behind me and hung her quilt next to mine. She'd put the words Refuge by the Sea across the top. I read the title out loud.

"That's why Asilomar supposedly means," she said. "Even though it's kind of a made up word."

She snaked her arm through mine and hugged my shoulder. I leaned into her. We'd really enjoyed our time together. She and Harriet were already planning a fall trip to the Bay Area. I looked forward to seeing them again.

Our wall hangings looked nothing alike, although our themes were the same. Her quilt featured the people of Asilomar, with pictures of the original YMCA girls, the Stuck-ups, the Pirates, including her grandfather. She had just finished adding thread to the surface, outlining the curves of the faces and filling in the shadows.

Mine was a landscape, bordered by the half square triangle blocks. It was one giant Ocean Waves block with my appliqué in the middle. Cinnamon had taught me well. I'd expanded the traditional block and added my own touches to it.

I had come here to learn, and I had. Not exactly what I'd thought I would learn, but that was okay.

A horn beeped outside. I looked out the window in time to see a pickup with the Pellicano Construction logo on the door go by. Kevin, with Kym in the passenger seat. She was facing him, her hands gesturing. I figured her mouth was going, too. Probably nonstop since he'd arrived in the middle of the night. I caught a glimpse of her tightly covered head and his flip hand wave before they turned onto the road that would lead them north.

Buster was hanging out in the Administration building, playing pool with Tony. We were having dinner with Tony's new girlfriend. I couldn't wait to meet the girl who'd brought my brother back to civilization. Then Buster and I would go home. We'd put our golfing weekend off for a few weeks. I wanted to check in with my dad, and QP, and sleep in my own bed. With Buster at my side.

Ursula had made it safely to my house and went to work this morning at the store. Vangie said that within her first hour at QP, Ursula had made a five-hundred dollar sale, helping two sisters pick out fabric for their queen-sized quilts. Ina had taken her home and put her in her spare room. Ina's work at the women's shelter, Women First, meant Ursula would have access to counseling and job training. With Paul gone, she finally had the opportunity to create a new life for herself. Out in the open. I was hoping she'd stay on with me, working at the store. She might be what QP needed.

"What do you want this quilt to be, Dewey?" Cinnamon asked. She'd come around behind me again.

"What do you mean?"

"Do you want it to represent your time here at Asilomar?"

I laughed. "Are you suggesting I add a crouching mountain lion? Or maybe my brother and his rifle," I said, feeling the pain only after the words were out. It was too early to joke.

She was gentle as always, but firm. "You don't need to be literal."

I laughed. "Good thing because I don't want a quilt with a gun in the middle of it."

She ignored my lame attempt. "Try this. Close your eyes. Think about the last five days. What part of that do you want to take forward with you? This quilt could serve as a reminder of what you learned this week."

I was still thinking literally. "You mean, like how you taught me to make a quilt

331

block expand and make it look different?" I was proud of my one Ocean Waves block. Cinnamon had taught me to look at traditional blocks in a new way.

She shook her head, her braid landing on her back, laid her hand on my chest. "What you learned in here."

I felt her warm palm, heard her bracelets tinkle. In here, I thought. In my heart.

"Close your eyes and tell me what you see."

I settled back in my chair as she walked away. The first pictures that came up were sad ones. Mercedes, Paul Wiggins, Quentin. All gone.

I shifted into something more serene. The blue ocean, lacy waves, black rocks. The tide pools with their secrets just under the surface. Pelicans splashing down. The dunes ever shifting but sustaining life.

I remembered time spent outdoors with Buster and felt myself smile.

The pictures I took of the Julia Morgan buildings came up next. The bare beams in the Pirates' Den and the Stuck-Up Inn. The elegant repeat of the roof trusses in Merrill Hall. The great stone fireplace wall in the Administration building. The way the buildings embraced their natural habitat and faced the elements, exposed but strong.

I heard a funny noise and opened my eyes. Buster was standing near the window, trying to get my attention. I laughed as he silently pleaded with me to join him, on bended knee with his hands in a beseeching pose.

I went outside. "What," I said, mock sternly. His eyes twinkled and I felt myself getting lost in them.

"I saw a raccoon. I had to make sure you were all right," he said. His cheeks were twitching from restraining his laughter.

"I'm a big girl," I said, catching his face in my hands and looking into his eyes. "I can fight off the fierce raccoons."

He caught my waist and kissed me. "I know you can," he said. "It's why I love you so."

"Come back for me in two hours," I said, pushing him away.

I watched him walk off, and waved when he turned to see if I'd gone back inside.

He'd apologized all night for going hunting for the mountain lion with Tony and not being around when I needed him. I told him it was okay. I was fine on my own. I loved being with him, and I would always want to be with him, but I could make it alone.

I'd found out that I could withstand evil and not lose myself to it. I could yield to the forces beyond my control, help where I could and give up what I couldn't. I had no way of knowing Paul was following me, trying to get to Ursula. His inability to let go of Ursula had gotten him killed. Quentin's attachment to the Rose Box, to what he thought was his inheritance had led him to a bitter end as well. Even the mountain lion, unable to control her nature, had met death.

I needed to remember that to not change was to die. I had to acknowledge what was missing. I'd fired Kym and then tried to move on as though nothing had happened. I'd missed Tony in my life, but never acknowledged the hole his absence meant in my life.

Back in the classroom, I flipped through the pictures I'd taken on my laptop. One image stopped as the slideshow stuttered.

I'd taken a picture of a cypress tree, its branches sculpted by the wind into a structure that didn't resemble a tree anymore. The branches had bent almost at a ninety-degree angle and looked frozen. It sat among a group of similar trees, but was set apart. Perhaps the tree planted closest to it had died.

It was beautiful. Adjusting to the forces greater than itself, but thriving.

This was the final element my quilt

needed. The cypress represented what I wanted to be. Open to the elements, but able to bend and change. Able to grow despite forces around it that were stunting its growth. Able to withstand forces of evil and still remain my essential self.

ABOUT THE AUTHOR

Terri Thayer is busy writing, quilting, and keeping an eye out for murderers at quilt shows. So as not to disappoint her fans, she is still trying to figure out a way to bring Buster to the guild's show-and-tell.

We hope you have enjoyed this Large Print book. Other Thorndike, Wheeler, Kennebec, and Chivers Press Large Print books are available at your library or directly from the publishers.

For information about current and upcoming titles, please call or write, without obligation, to:

Publisher
Thorndike Press
295 Kennedy Memorial Drive
Waterville, ME 04901
Tel. (800) 223-1244

or visit our Web site at:

http://gale.cengage.com/thorndike

OR

Chivers Large Print
published by BBC Audiobooks Ltd
St James House, The Square
Lower Bristol Road
Bath BA2 3SB
England
Tel. +44(0) 800 136919
email: bbcaudiobooks@bbc.co.uk
www.bbcaudiobooks.co.uk

All our Large Print titles are designed for easy reading, and all our books are made to last.